Widely admired as the godfa[...] **Derek Raymond** was born [...] of a textile magnate, he dropped [...] of [...] aged sixteen and spent much of his early career among criminals. The Factory series followed his early novels, *The Crust on Its Uppers* and *A State of Denmark* (both published by Serpent's Tail). His literary memoir *The Hidden Files* was published in 1992. He died in London in 1994.

Serpent's Tail are reissuing the Factory novels: *He Died with His Eyes Open* is already available.

Praise for *The Crust on Its Uppers*

'Few novels chronicle so lovingly the life and mores of 1960s London… Britain's class system was changing. Cook, the old Etonian, takes us to card-grafters in Peckham and rent collectors along the Balls Pond Road; to greasy Gloucester Road caffs and jellied-eel stalls in Whitechapel… Confession is a fashionable literary genre these days. But this younger breed of confessors, well, you can tell they are fibbing sometimes, can't you? Not so Cook; *The Crust on Its Uppers* is the kosher article by a man who was on the down-escalator all his life' *Sunday Times*

'Raymond's autobiographical account of the dodgy transactions between high-class wide boys and low-class villains. You won't read a better novel about '60s London' *i-D*

'Tremendous black comedy of Chelsea gangland' *The Face*

'Peopled by a fast-talking shower of queens, spades, morries, slags, shysters, grifters, and grafters of every description, it is one of the great London novels' *New Statesman*

NIGHTMARE
IN THE STREET

Derek Raymond

A complete catalogue record for this book
can be obtained from the British Library on request

The right of Derek Raymond to be identified as the author of this work
has been asserted in accordance with the Copyright, Designs and Patents
Act 1988

First published in 1988 by Editions Rivages, Paris

First published in the UK in 2006 by Serpent's Tail,
4 Blackstock Mews, London N4 2BT
Website: www.serpentstail.com

ISBN 1 85242 908 9
ISBN 978 1 85242 908 9

Printed by Mackays of Chatham plc

10 9 8 7 6 5 4 3 2 1

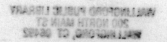

To Gisèle, of course.

1

Kleber was a plain-clothes copper; he worked for the Police Judiciare out of police station number 50, Boulevard de Sébastopol. He was born in Paris, though his family came from Alsace-Lorraine, and he was forty, married, but with no children, though God knows they tried hard enough. He was neither a nice man nor a nasty one, as far as he knew, but was simply a detective, and a smooth, swift and efficient one with a good brain, though it was true that he had a sharp tongue that kept him well down in the ranks, as his colleagues could testify, and could be very unpleasant to unpleasant people—the thieves, pimps and murderers he was paid to catch. He wasn't a violent man—indeed what surprised everyone around him, including himself, was his capacity for feeling and love, an element that his work caused him to keep mostly in check as a man does with a big dog on a leash that dashes after every scent when going for a run in the park on Saturday morning.

Far back and long ago, when he had been so small that he now found it hard to remember (his growth, youth and career having practically effaced his childhood and both his parents now being dead), there was still a part of him that recalled his infancy: his parents' stuffy bedroom on the second floor of a block of flats, an old block on a street between Nation and Vincennes. There was still a part of him that was always his earliest childhood, nerves in him that responded to the cheap curtains they had managed to find and put up in the room during some suffocating post-war summer. He remembered those curtains, in whose pattern he seemed to discern letters of the alphabet, the Lord's Prayer printed by his mother in block capitals and glued above his bed (they were Protestants), the faces, some friendly, others less so, marked out by cracks in the plaster, and the boiling or freezing streets outside the block when his mother took him out shopping. Sometimes he could still quite clearly reconstruct in his heart and mind nights when his mother and father had taken him, squalling, into their bed and heated or cooled him according to his needs, talked to him, sometimes sung to him and soothed him to sleep. He had no idea then, and had been born too late ever really to understand, that his parents had been very brave people during the war, had been imprisoned and tortured for it; nor, no matter how much he read about those events afterwards, could he ever truly understand what the foreign soldiers, strolling about in Paris, and whose photographs he often stared at, symbolised, nor what they stood for and had done.

That all took a very long time to penetrate him and, by the time it had, he had left school and was already planning to join the police; and it was with surprise that he heard his mother telling him one day how, at the time her brother had died when he, Kleber, was nine, he had turned his face to the wall and remained in bed for ten days without sleeping, eating or moving. That was a shock that it must have been more convenient for him to forget—it must have been, at that age, either a question of his forgetting it or his destruction.

Why the police? Kleber often said to his friend Mark that it must have been in answer to his being stricken that soon by family losses; that he had embarked on a violent career as some strange compensation for that other, earlier violence. Mark perfectly understood because, as a criminal, he was in a violent career himself. They were both the same age and had been to school together. They had always got on very well; there had never been a cross word between them, and they had frequently protected each other in the street.

Kleber didn't care much for daylight; he never had, he did most of his work in the dark. He had certain intense dislikes. He loathed harshly lit bores quacking away at their own parties (though his job obliged him to listen to them sometimes), and he didn't like accepting little cakes from overdressed women. He didn't like to have family photograph albums forced on him by people who were forced to like children, nor being accorded over-ready handshakes and kisses when he knew perfectly well that, as a stranger, he had no right to either.

The only people he liked were real people, which was why he had never got at all far in his career—but the terrible thing about Kleber was that he didn't care.

It was always the same battle for Kleber. He didn't entirely know how he had got into it, but that didn't change anything, modify anything. For some reason he was always on his own, fighting for both the living and the dead, the visible and the invisible—the dead were always as real to him as the living, especially when they were wrongly dead.

It was often painful to him to have to wake up every morning, coughing his lungs out after too many drinks, cigarettes (he smoked fifty a day), and too many interviews with people the day before who were completely lost both to and in themselves—and his work, he found, got harder as it went on. Of course it was easy for him to be tough in a way; he had been brought up hard and had learned very early how to put street values into street language. He could get hold of a deviator, if he had to, by his wrist, his fingers or his neck and break any of them. He disliked firearms and never carried them if he could help it, even though he was fast with a pistol. Unless he was confronted with violence he never used it, preferring to find the man he was looking for in some street or a bar, as a result of patient enquiry: 'I've got a few questions to put to you over a certain matter, darling.'

Yet Kleber often had doubts about what he was doing, or rather how it ought to be done, but the trouble was there weren't many solutions. All the same, this was a discussion Mark and he often raised together, the question of why crime existed, not where it was. They both agreed that friendship outclassed all laws; a shielded look could be given in a street that meant many times more than a bullet or a textbook. They also both of them always held that liberty was a secret matter because it was so pure: you could no more place a value on it than on wrought gold unburied from a different age.

'It's like yesterday once you see it.'

'Yes, but it's unbelievably old, far older than our modern race.'

They also frequently discussed a central question—what was the value of a human life? As they ate together in restaurants they came back to that over again; to both criminal and policeman it seemed to them to be the only question.

'After all, we're friends; how much do we really matter to each other?'

'I suppose we won't find out about that until one or the other of us is dead.'

One night Kleber said: 'Don't be a fool. It'll be too late by then, and so the question'll never be settled.' And he signalled to the waiter to bring them another bottle of wine.

'Don't you think it's idiotic for us to be cast in opposite roles?'

'Yes, of course,' said Mark, 'yet how could either of us have helped it?'

'Christ, if I knew the answer to that,' said Kleber, 'I'd know the answer to everything.'

And so, to Kleber, it was always the brilliance of a previous age that troubled and moved him, in part because he seemed to have discovered it through his earliest memories, and he found he responded to it without really knowing why. It was the same as knowing something without being able to prove it, and the logical part of him didn't care for things like that at all.

Not yet, at least.

The business with Kleber's wife, Elenya, was typical of his friendship with Mark, not that it was a friendship that needed any cementing—he was thinking of the night when Mark, going down the Rue St-Denis in a car just after Kleber had first met her, automatically stopped when he saw her being beaten up on the pavement, so that that turned out to be a beating-up that went entirely the other way. They sometimes spoke about that night and Mark, who had never had a settled life with any woman, was at first so excited to know that Kleber had experienced what he had never had that he once said that it was as if he himself were part of their lives, whereon

Derek Raymond

Kleber answered, 'Of course,' and poured him another glass of Bordeaux, adding: 'You silly bastard.' For because of that act of Mark's, Kleber owed him a debt, although, because they had both of them known each other so long, neither of them consciously thought of it as a debt. But both of them knew that if either were threatened, the other would descend on the guilty person like a predator, from a great height. Mark had paid his debt so that now he, Kleber, was in reserve, police or no police. Kleber would see to it that anyone who threatened Mark's life would pay for that with his own.

So our society, for all its mediocrity and corruption, is still occasionally based on the absolute of our common soul, and a human being can at times be as strong as God.

Once, when they were eating together, Kleber said half-jokingly: 'It's no use being frightened of shadows, is it?'

'If we were frightened of them, we'd be frightened of everything, wouldn't we, and that would never do.'

Kleber said: 'Do you remember that winter morning, we must have been sixteen, staying with my grandfather, and he gave us that little gun and told us to go up to those huts behind the house where he kept his rabbits and shoot the rats?'

'Sure, we got fourteen of them.'

'I used to hate rats. I was frightened of them.'

'Me too. But what fun it was once the sun got up properly and we could see them in the corners running up the walls as we pulled the bales of straw out.'

'Looking round you now, in this city,' said Kleber, 'nothing much seems to have changed about the rats, does it?'

'Have some more Beaujolais.'

12

Evenings like these are important, Kleber thought, putting his fork aside and staring into his newly filled glass; they're worth all the difficult, nauseating ones. He said: 'Do you remember Lucienne?'

'The blonde girl we both had such fun with? How could I forget?'

'You remember what happened to her?'

'We were at school together.'

'And after that?'

'She threw herself out of a window. Or was she thrown out? We'll never know. We should have put a stop to that before it started.'

'I know we should,' said Kleber. 'But we didn't.'

'I remember the day it happened as though it were yesterday. I was held up talking and didn't hear the news until I got in.'

'I've somehow managed to put it out of my mind,' said Kleber. 'At times anyway.'

'It still comes back to me and you, though.'

'Well, I find it does,' said Kleber. 'Guilt never leaves go of you, does it?'

'How could it? There she was, pretty girl, gave us both everything she had, her face, her laughter, her body in fine weather, and what did we do?'

'Let her drop out of a fucking window,' Kleber said.

'You're always on a seesaw,' said Mark, 'no matter who you are or what you're doing.'

'I know,' said Kleber, 'only once people have gone there's no means of getting them back again, and there was no seesaw about the way she hit the street.'

'I can't really accept that it was our fault.'

'I can,' said Kleber. 'I easily can—now. I'm not speaking for you, but as far as I was concerned I simply let her drop where she didn't suit me.' He added: 'And she did drop. Four floors.'

'Ignorance isn't murder.'

'Yes, it is,' said Kleber. 'It has the same result.' He called to the waiter, who was passing: 'Two coffees and two large Armagnacs.'

When they arrived, Mark dropped a lump of sugar into his coffee and stirred it. He said: 'Do you remember the day of the aeroplane? It was the time I had that British stripped-down Triumph 6, and you, she and I took a ride right out into the fields beyond Pontoise. The pilot circled above us, watching out of his cockpit, wanting to come down and join in our antics, only he couldn't find a place to land, the corn was too thick.'

'It was a wonderful day,' said Kleber. 'She loved it.'

'Yes,' said Mark, 'but I don't think either of us really understood how much.'

'The trouble is,' said Kleber, 'that you and I are so used to pain that perhaps we no longer really feel it.'

'I hope you're right,' said Mark. 'I'm a villain, but I can't say I've ever got used to pain.'

'I remember how you and I both hunted her in that corn,' said Kleber. 'It was August. We could hear her laughing in it but we couldn't find her, and then we did and we all had a picnic and sunbathed.'

'Seeing what happened to Lucienne,' Mark said, 'are you afraid of what's to come?'

'Yes, I am,' said Kleber. 'You know, on the one hand my job is to interrogate deviators. I pick them up, say to them: "I'm not remotely interested in your blag, darling—the form you've got, you could be doing a hundred handsprings in hell for all I cared." And then, on the other hand, I've got Elenya, whom I adore and worship, and there are times when I feel an abyss between my work and my feelings. I sometimes feel I haven't the equipment to bridge the gap; I'm an ordinary man, after all.'

'And that's why we tend to suffer ordinary fates,' Mark said, 'and the trouble with ordinary fates is that, like Lucienne's, they can be extremely painful and very seldom noticed, if at all. She was lucky that she had the two of us to go to her funeral, at least.'

'I don't see what's lucky about being dead,' Kleber said.

Kleber decided that he didn't really know what he was all about, in the end. Elenya meant everything to him, and he believed he was well able to protect her, he was sure of that—although at times he had terrible doubts and dreams which, as he was to find out, were well grounded. Those times when he was with her at night he swam in that ocean of uneasy sleep beside her which gives no relief and is as exhausting as the shallow day that comes after it. Bores, buses, work, interminable phone calls—he didn't feel that life in the big cities was what he was for.

But the irony was that he had been born in a big city, and was thought by his superiors to be very good at working in them.

Yet at some point he had revolted against mediocrity and corruption. When was it that he had been first struck by the majority of his colleagues' shallow attitude towards the truth of an affair, he asked himself. Wasn't it when he had first taken Elenya, a being from that world opposite to his, unresisting in his arms? Wasn't it through her that he had first placed a total value on a human being—not by forcing her but by knowing her; not just by having someone but by being accepted by her? His knowledge of Elenya had utterly changed his view of existence as it had been before they were together. His need of her was so constant even now, after four years, that it made him start to bleed inside every time he thought of her.

But he had to go on being in the police because it was his career, and even now he still believed somewhere that being in the police was worth while. He continued to hope that his efforts in it were not entirely for nothing, just as he knew that the mysteries of existence would never be revealed. He often said to himself with a shrug that merely by being born he had signed a contract with the earth, not all of whose clauses he had been able or been given time to read—you had to interpret what you had signed as you went along, and hope it didn't get you: he, Elenya, everybody, they were all to some extent in that situation, and therefore all bonded to an elusive quality in life which returned insidiously no matter how often you broke it.

But what had all that to do with Elenya's body, which magnetised him to her as none other could? It had nothing to do with the way she slipped into bed with him on one of his rare nights off, or how she later closed him into her with her arms and her being.

And so he was marked off as one of those difficult coppers who loved his wife, dined with a villain who had been a schoolmate and took a completely different view of justice to the Ministry of the Interior, which was why he had just hit a police inspector in the face for interfering in a murder after Kleber had categorically warned him not to, and that was why he had been suspended until further notice on full pay.

2

Kleber had heard—because in his job he heard everything—that some people, certain people who were not spotless themselves, described his wife Elenya as that little Polish whore; but nobody, nobody at all, had ever said it to his face, not after the first, which was also the last time. That had been settled out on dark ground, and the man who had passed the remark to Kleber's face had decided, when he got out of hospital, to go back to Lyons after all and live there permanently.

It wasn't Elenya's fault she was a whore; if you like, it was her face's fault. She was far too beautiful and well made for the quarter she grew up in: the concrete blocks dotted about with their sweating walls, murdered by bureaucrats and heavy machinery where villages had once stood; that was the kind of place where she was born. Her birth dumped her into despair, unemployment and that collapse in relationships between neighbours that occurs when no one has any work or any money except for that endless haggle for a cheque with the Social Security.

But that wasn't Elenya's fault. Her error was to be beautiful and far too well developed at fourteen, and so her father raped her at that age. It began as a good-night cuddle when he came into her room (something she hated him doing anyway) one Saturday night drunk, and ended with her shrieks and his self-murdering tears after he had had his half-hard way with her and dribbling little orgasm—she had already started to have other

17

dreams for herself in life which her father, by that act, appeared to have stabbed at birth.

Her father liked to tell people down at the bar that, though self-educated, he was a well-educated man. But he was full of shit. He had been a clerk in a local electronics factory who was fired for his absurd fussiness, telling too many people what to do all the time when in fact he was practically at the bottom of the ladder there. So he was called in one Friday night, given his cards and money and told to get lost, after which he never got another job and no wonder—he was forty-five already and looked older. He liked to sit and look mysterious in an acrylic armchair in the sitting room of their horrible eleventh-floor flat, and it wasn't difficult—he had no competition except his wife, who never listened to him but talked to the wall about curtains, eiderdowns and the monetary value of things, and whether they oughtn't to be saving for a new telly like the people on the floor downstairs had.

Yes, Elenya's mother was a great gabbler—but dangerous because she was only half-stupid. She was harmless for as long as she could talk without interruption; she had a long, loose mouth, the shape of some shallow river, and any old rubbish would come pouring out of it, from telling tales about neighbours that she had half-understood to bargains that she had read about—aloud—in the junk mail that was poked through their door. She went on talking even in bed, and so never had time to let Dad have it, shrugging him off her, preferring to go on talking even in her sleep—something that drove everyone else on her floor crazy since her head rested against the partition wall which the municipal authorities, so as to save money that they could put into their own pockets, had built especially thin. But she got naughty when she had no one to talk to.

And so Dad came into his daughter's room that night—however, the trouble was that Mother caught him at it, hearing the child's cries, which were loud enough to pierce even her monologue, and so the father, aware of the door opening to the light in the passage, turned to see her stout shape screaming obscenities at him and he staggered upright, buttoning himself up. Elenya got out of that little concrete hell and went to stay with a school friend, saying nothing to anybody, and kneeling to God to plead that she wasn't pregnant. A lot of rationalisation went on between the parents of which the central point was that, as Mum couldn't hope to get her new telly without Dad's cheque from Social Security, it was Elenya who had to go; besides, that removed temptation out of his way.

So Elenya had to go, and go she did—on the streets, because her parents had kicked her out without a penny; it happened to thousands of teenage girls every year, all over Europe. She soon learned to be unhappy, how to mask it with a cold face and a sharp tongue. But neither expressed her true personality, which was a very attractive gentle one, and sometimes the strain between her real face and her false one became too great for her. Still, there was a cure for that too: she quickly found that you could almost, though not quite, manufacture happiness for yourself in bars, which was where she spent most of the little money that her pimp let her keep—it's such a banal story until it happens to you. And so she would probably have gone on like that if her pimp, who was on cocaine as well as pushing it, hadn't killed a punter who couldn't pay, so that it was Kleber's duty, as well as pleasure, to do him for murder. Elenya was with the pimp when Kleber arrived with the warrant, and that was how they met. She had to go to the station and make a statement, though she hadn't been a witness to the killing, and he took to ringing her at her flat after that. He managed also to get her excluded from the case altogether, for which she was grateful; and they found themselves meeting in the bars that they both used for their own reasons, too, and one night Kleber asked her to come and eat with him, and they talked for such a long time that even though it was a restaurant that didn't shut until one, they suddenly found that the staff were putting the chairs upside down on the tables to sweep up. A great rush of feeling such as Kleber hadn't known since he was sixteen carried him away, and he realised that he was in love with her and that she felt the same.

So they both got into a taxi and he took her back to his place, where he put her into a spare room that he had, for he felt far too deeply to just tip her over on her back like that.

'I'm a drain on you,' she said. 'Financially, I mean.'

'Don't be so silly,' said Kleber. 'I'm a man on my own. I can earn plenty of money for both of us.'

'I love you.'

'Same here,' said Kleber.

She said she was afraid to go back now to the streets and bars where he had met her (it was the quarter where she liked to go shopping because she knew it so well) in case some of her pimp's friends decided to have a go at her, particularly now she was going out with a copper. But Kleber told her not be afraid; he explained to her that she ran no risk. He went to see a mate of his on the Vice Squad, and any troubles she might have expected to run into were very swiftly looked after.

3

After they had been living together for some time she took him home to see her parents, and he listened silently while each of them rattled on at him in their different ways. Kleber knew about their story from Elenya, of course—but they didn't know his, and somehow Kleber just didn't take the trouble to tell them. The mother he dismissed at once as a fool and selfish with it—but he didn't like the dad at all, not only because he knew what the man had done to his daughter but because, as a copper, to Kleber he had all the makings of a grass or even worse, although to Kleber, apart from a killer, there wasn't anything much worse. He, too, had a swollen ego; it burst like liver through a stomach wound in the face of what he took to be Kleber's stupid silence. He finally got round to asking Kleber what he did for a living; Kleber told him he was a cab driver, and the father began telling him how he could really do better at it, if Kleber worked as hard in life as he had himself. Kleber thought of one of the things, as he watched Elenya moving about in the adjacent kitchen, that her father worked hard at, apart from a bottle. The man's eyes were set too close to his nose, which was long; he had a wet, unpleasant mouth, too, from which foam constantly rattled as he spoke through his cracked teeth. He was as neatly dressed as if he had a job to go to every morning, and was extremely careful not to get any ash on himself from the occasional cigarette he smoked, the ends of which were always sodden. His gaze also darted constantly to the bottle of Scotch Kleber had brought to see how far the level had gone down, so Kleber went out of his way to help himself liberally to it. He had a great deal to say about politics to which Kleber didn't reply, though he gathered that the left had no chance whatsoever of getting a vote from him. In the end Kleber said: 'Your opinions don't matter, Mr Kucharski.'

'I'd have you know I've spent my whole life educating myself!' he shouted.

'Your vote?' said Kleber. 'You might as well try to stop an express train with your foot.'

It was the first time Kleber had said anything definite and there was quite a long silence after it.

Mrs Kucharski tried to start talking about the price of electric wall clocks, but her husband, without even turning to look at her, simply said: 'Shut up.' He said to Kleber: 'What do you want with our daughter, then?'

'I want to marry her,' said Kleber.

'What? Our only child marry a cab driver?'

'There are worse trades than being a cab driver,' said Kleber, 'and I'm a very hard-working one.'

'Why aren't you out driving now, then?'

'Because I work days,' said Kleber. 'Anyway, as to Elenya, we love each other, and I want to be with her, virgin that she is, where no other man's ever been before. As a father, you must appreciate that.'

He was glad now that he had arranged with Elenya to keep out of the way while he talked to them.

Kucharski tried to go on looking at Kleber, but his head wobbled about, and he couldn't help himself turning an odd colour. 'I don't know. You'll find her a difficult girl.'

'Really?" said Kleber. 'I wonder why? We've been

going out for some time together and I've never found her difficult at all.'

'She errs in her ways,' said Mrs Kucharski.

'Perhaps she's a lost sheep,' said Kleber, 'though I've no sense of knowing whose fault that might be, if she is.'

'Are you trying to be clever or something?' Kucharski said.

'No,' said Kleber. 'The harder you try to be clever, the less you succeed. You're the proof of it, Mr Kucharski.'

Kucharski turned white. 'I don't like you,' he whispered. Kleber thought it might have been the first time he had ever whispered.

'The plain truth is,' said Kleber, 'that you and your wife kicked your daughter out of your home for some reason, and I don't think either of you are in any position to look down your noses because she's going to marry a cab driver.'

'Do you love her?' said Mrs Kucharski suddenly.

'I've never loved anyone so much in my life,' said Kleber, 'not even my parents, who are dead, and whom I loved a very great deal.'

Kucharski sat looking at his wife in stunned silence; Kleber wondered if he was praying that she wouldn't go on talking about love.

'Do you believe you know what love is?' said Mrs Kucharski.

'Do you know?' said Kleber. 'Does your husband?'

Kucharski pursed his wet little lips and shook his head. 'I don't know about you and our girl. I myself don't like you; no, my mind's not satisfied about you yet by a long way; no, I'm not at all sure.'

'Well, that can't be helped,' said Kleber, standing up. 'I'm perfectly sure, and so is Elenya—why don't you ask her?'

But Kucharski didn't have to because, as Kleber spoke, Elenya came in through the kitchen door and stood on the horrid sitting room carpet with her hands on her hips and said: 'I love him, and after all you've both done for me that's all either of you need worry about, except yourselves.'

She hadn't spoken loudly, but the effect of her words produced a long, ringing silence into which Kucharski, in the end, said feebly: 'She's very young to be married.'

'Better than being too old,' said Kleber. He looked at his watch and said to Elenya: 'Well, that's all. It's supper time; I'm hungry. We'll go out to eat. Are you ready?'

'Coming,' she said, and turned to pick up her coat.

Kleber said to her parents: 'Say good night to the future Mrs Kleber,' and they did say it, Kucharski glistening with sweat.

4

The trouble Kleber was having at work had to do with a murder case he had been on. Outside the police, only Elenya knew about it, because neither of them ever had any secrets from each other. At the same time, even as he spoke to her about it, he was dreadfully disturbed, the more so for its being in a way that he couldn't name; it was a fear he had in his soul when he looked at her that there was no real reason for, and that made it worse. The night it blew up he went out into the bathroom and looked hard into the mirror, trying to remember himself exactly as he had been as a child, only to find that his face had been altered by his work.

'You need character lines on your face,' his own father had said to him once; 'otherwise they won't believe you at interviews. You've got to be practically like publicity in front of these people on the board, pretend you're selling cigarettes on television. Never mind if you've never had the experience; pretend you've had it.'

What force, thought Kleber, caused all our births in order to ensure our fall? He said to himself that these were absurd questions to ask of oneself, of anybody; yet he found them necessary, though not at all fashionable.

He had known at once when he joined the police that the battle he was going to have to obtain natural justice was going to have to be fought against most of his colleagues. There were so many bits of what he had experienced that he couldn't swallow—shades of old wars, suffering; he didn't see why he shouldn't ask the

25

questions. Men, after all, had done it under rifle fire. If they could do it, he thought to himself, I can do it. I've seen, on film, men shot against a wall for what they believed; they fell without a word. But it was the executioners who were spat on by the people, once the people had regained the strength to speak; not the victims. Bravery in a rotten climate is hurriedly buried, Kleber thought, and I must balance this while I'm part of this earth.

Kleber had already solved the murder; it was a matter of a girl who had had lead popped into her face by a boyfriend, and it had been his job to find out which one of her boyfriends had pulled the trigger on her. Kleber had found him all right, and taken the boy through his usual patient questioning. There was dreadful suffering on the assassin's part, but there would have had to be anyway, no matter how the truth came out. It sounded simple, but of course such things as violent death can never be. After taking him quietly over and over the ground (why had he split her head open with a bullet?), Kleber found out through the boy's tears that it was because, as with so many men, he felt his virility was at stake, and he became convinced that she was two-timing him with his best friend; the two always played darts together and went to the Saturday match. He had become so drunk with her one night, so disgraced and disgusted in his spirit, that he had somehow staggered up to the great question as a man might under fire and asked whether she thought he was a man, and she laughed at him in that way women do at times, not understanding or forgetting about men; and she said no, she didn't think he was a man, since she was pissed too;

she thought the whole thing very funny, which he didn't.

And so he went and got the gun and shot her, carelessly almost, in a different state.

'You know,' he said to Kleber, 'it was some kind of sick jealousy that made me do it, and she would keep comparing me with her other lays; she told me I was so dull compared with the others; she told me how she hated people clinging to me the way I did to her. You know,' he said, moving fitfully on his bed in the remand cell, 'I'm not really dull, no duller than anyone else— anyway, I usen't to be. Of course, I'm dull now, after what's happened, after what I did; it kind of makes you dull. But what's the point? OK, she's dead and I killed her; what more do you want?'

Behind the police façade, thinking of Elenya, Kleber really didn't know, but said to this distracted man: 'I don't think you'll go down hard. Just hard enough to teach you not to go killing people again.'

The boy said: 'You can't know what love means, to say anything so stupid. The shock of the bullet is for oneself, not just for anyone.'

Kleber had seen the photos of the girl; it was a shallow face. Even in death, spilled over herself, she had no depth. Take away the white jeans and top they'd found her in and you'd got a young female bore without an original idea in her head. The half-wink she'd had for Kleber as a dead woman proved nothing to him. Actually, it wasn't so much a wink he had seen in her face when called to the flat as a sly expression, as much as to say: darkness is cheap; how much of it do you think you can stand?

Working with death is like working with insanity; it takes courage and practice. If he had had neither, Kleber would have vomited when he saw her face, the more so when he looked at the boy that he had to charge and saw how mortally overruled he had been by his act in his heart and mind.

It was all a matter, Kleber thought, of putting everything in its proper light. It was a glaring, real light, too much so for most people's eyes. He looked at the wretched survivor of this slaughter sitting there in the remains of his nice suit, having blasted out of his middle-class home. He recited to himself as if he, too, were in a different world:

> 'Solomon Grundy,
> Born on Monday,
> Got drunk on Tuesday,
> Fell ill on Wednesday,
> Worse on Thursday,
> Shriven on Friday,
> Died on Saturday,
> Buried on Sunday,
> And that was the end of Solomon Grundy.'

Kleber got the boy down to the station and was met by this inspector he most hated, a fat, jolly-looking man whose good humour stopped at his eyes; with him and Kleber the hatred was mutual. 'Well, don't tell me,' said the individual. 'You've got him at last, have you? Been through plenty of philosophy and stuff? We're actually going to charge him at long last, are we?'

'I am,' said Kleber. 'Not you, darling.'

'Oh, I've got nothing to do right now,' said the other one. 'It might be rather fun just to lend a hand. It's a straight murder, is it?'

'No,' said Kleber, looking at him with a slow fuse in his

eyes, 'this is manslaughter with mitigating circumstances, and I'm looking after it. Now fuck off. Nobody ordered you.'

'Mitigating circumstances?' said the inspector, grinning. 'This little child here blew her to bits, didn't he? I've seen the photos. Blew her swede practically off! What mitigating circumstances? Here, there's an empty cell downstairs; I've just emptied it on another case.'

Kleber put the boy he had arrested behind him and said to the inspector: 'Get out of here. You've had your card well marked. Never interfere with my cases. I've told you before, I've warned you.'

'Oh, come on,' he said. 'Give me just ten minutes alone with your little gladiator, and I'll burst him wide open, sweetheart. I think I'll take this over now.'

'He's making his statement to me,' Kleber said, 'and no one else. Now get off, do you hear?'

'Are you threatening me, sergeant?'

'No,' said Kleber. 'I'm just fending you off with the end of my boot.'

The inspector came at Kleber with the flat of his hand straight to his face, but Kleber let him pass and kicked one of his knees out. Before his opponent could go down Kleber straightened him in his fall, broke his nose and knocked three of his front teeth out. They were quite small teeth, really, with blood on the ends of them; they lay on the cement floor between Kleber and the man whom Kleber was about to charge with manslaughter. The inspector lay doubled up moaning in a corner, and why not?

Kleber picked up the phone in the room and told the sergeant who answered to come and take away what was left of the inspector.

Kleber was amazed to find that he didn't care about

29

what he had done to this horrible man. He even patted on the shoulder the man whom he had just arrested for the murder of his girlfriend. 'I thought life was bad enough outside,' said the latter, 'but now I'm not sure.'

'Keep on not being sure,' said Kleber, 'and you'll be as unsteady as any of us. Now let's go into another office where we can be quiet, and try to get all this business into some kind of shape—like sorted out, if you know what I mean.'

Walking down the corridor behind the young murderer, Kleber thought perhaps he should have felt sorry about what he had just done to his own career, but somehow he found that he couldn't manage it.

While Kleber was waiting to be suspended, he charged the boy himself in the presence of two other officers as if nothing abnormal had happened—after all, it was he who had made the arrest. He saw to it himself that the whole scene was quiet, informal, human almost, and when the paperwork was over Kleber took the young man to his cell and went in and sat with him for a while. Afterwards, when his prisoner had fallen back on the grey army bed, Kleber went upstairs to his office; some young flies were quarrelling together on his open notebook.

5

Kleber's problem was that it was absolute in him: he had no fence he could sit on. With Kleber, people were either alive or dead, and in either case he wanted to know why, how and what for—it was the detective in him. For he had always believed that if you looked hard enough for the criminal, you would find God, and he had a good idea how merciless they both were. For God, like the criminal, was absent; each were brutes, and, thought Kleber, haven't we always worshipped cattle? Oh, intelligence, he thought, if I could only find it, Christ, don't I collect it. What a joy, he thought, walking along Sébastopol to be fired.

Kleber walked through the main glass doors of Commissariat No. 50, Boulevard de Sébastopol.

'Oh, well,' said the sergeant on duty, 'what a good thing you finally decided to drop by. Everyone here's been looking for you.'

'I know,' said Kleber. 'I perfectly well realise that.'

'Your boss particularly.'

'Good,' said Kleber. 'Excellent. When were things any different?'

'I've an idea they'll be different all right this time,' said the duty sergeant. 'Do you hand out bloody noses to inspectors like that every day?'

'Only if they fuck me about,' said Kleber.

'None of my business. I'm just handing you the

message.'

'People like you all do,' said Kleber. 'You're all like men who wear corsets in secret—you listen to all the gossip, far too much of it, but what's worse is you divide it by what you don't understand and pass it on.'

'You're going to be sacked,' said the sergeant. 'You must understand that.'

'Oh, yes,' said Kleber. 'All intelligent men are broken officers; they won't let us win our wars. Mind, it doesn't apply to you. I'm wasting even more of my time saying things like that to a uniformed doll like you; you'll be saying bollocks to the colonel next, won't you?'

'You'd better get upstairs and see them fast,' said the uniformed sergeant. 'They're there waiting for you, you know.'

'They always are,' said Kleber. 'But it's people like me who go into the minefield first.'

'I don't know what you're talking about.'

'I know,' said Kleber, 'and what's more, I didn't expect you to, darling—anyone can wear three stripes like you and push messages around.'

'I don't like the way you talk to people,' the sergeant said. 'I never have.'

Kleber bent over the desk and said to him very seriously: 'I can talk to you the way I do because I think you're a fake, pushing your bits of paper from one side of the plate to the other and drawing good wages for it from people who can't afford to pay them. Now reach for your gun.'

Kleber's was already in his hand, where it belonged; the other's was nowhere near his. 'You're too late,' said Kleber grimly, 'like all politicians and other clerks—but where I come from, out in the street, it all has to happen a great deal faster than that if you want to stay alive.' He put his gun away again; it was as if it had never appeared. 'I could have shot you down faster than a government if I'd wanted to, and you have the nerve to tell me what to do next?'

'So you don't give a fuck,' the uniformed man said.

'Not where people like you are concerned,' said Kleber. 'Why should I? You're not even able to kill me.'

He walked away to go upstairs. The entrance hall was full of number 50's morning taking—alcoholics, prostitutes who had been carved up by their pimps, people in once good clothes who had dined at Maxim's and then offered to do the washing-up when the bill came round, Arabs, negroes, whites who had lined their arm just once too often and who stood or sat there now, their eyes snowed out of their heads. One of them who caught Kleber's gaze was an American, young, with a guitar. He was sitting away in a corner on the pink and black tiles, his eyes as distinct as ice.

Our great capital, Kleber thought. He stopped to hear the American, who was singing:

'I'll tell you what it's all about;
It's about the myth that one day
There's going to be a dawn.
Like hell there'll be a dawn!
Throw some hope into yourself, man,
And get it inside yourself,
For there'll never be a dawn.
Meantime, now, all I want
Is to get this nightmare out of my arm
And these lights of Christ out of my mind.
Get it off, get it out of me—
I'm just a nightmare off from my arm,
A bad dream away from my arm.

Oh, get it out of me,
For I'm the nightmare just going into my arm.'

Kleber's English wasn't terrific, but that was the kind of language that knows no frontier, and he had done his work in the twilight land.

'Will we all see each other again when we're dead?' he wondered about the American as he made for the stairs. The uniformed police were already making everyone stand to get them into the blue wagons; Kleber picked his way through their wreckage, the wreckage of humanity itself.

His murderer had said: 'But I'm so mild. My parents always told me I was. Sandra, my girl, she always said that I was. Gentle. Did I really kill her? I can't believe it.'

'Well, she's dead,' said Kleber. 'You've got to face it.'

'Love makes you so soft,' the killer said.

'Until it turns to jealousy, yes,' said Kleber, 'and then look out.'

'I don't even remember taking my father's gun,' he said, 'because I was already in another state of mind. The person who killed Sandra was a person who looked and behaved like me. He was exactly like me, except that he stole and killed, things that as a bank clerk I myself would never do. I remember my father's house that night, the night I became someone else, the person I'd hidden, the person who'd got tired of it. He looked exactly like me, but he had nothing to do with me at all, because he had to—I mean, I had to—go to work the next morning and countersign other people's cheques. Meantime my precise image had to affirm and kill. Is what I'm saying sense or madness? Do you understand?'

'I think so,' said Kleber. 'Yes.'

'Everything was much too bright and dense,' said the

young man. 'The light in the room, the paint on the walls, the cut-price, fashionable furniture; all *he* remembered was exactly where to find the gun, and then how to steal the car from the people who had borne and criticised him. I tell you, it was like a dream. I only wanted to tell Sandra that she'd got it all wrong,' he said earnestly. 'It was like a family row that turned into something much worse suddenly. I knew that with my father's gun in my hands I could prove to her that I was a man, yet at the same time I remembered how painful, too bright, too thickly condensed in my head all those damned lights and colours in the room were as I pulled the trigger. I could have died after I'd done it—'

'Yes, I know,' said Kleber.

'How do you manage what you're not able to know?' implored the young man.

'I don't know myself,' said Kleber, 'except that somehow we all of us have to.'

'When she laughed at me,' he said, 'giggled at me the few times I came in her arms then you know what hell is.'

'It's all right,' said Kleber. 'Now just calm down; you know, we're not all monsters.'

'Mr Feeble,' he said, rocking back and forth on his prison bed, 'that's what she used to call me, and I would answer: there's no need to be so cruel—there are some things I can do that most people can't do, but no one person can do everything, Sandra, and do they honestly need to, darling, do you think?'

'Well, it turned out that you could kill,' said Kleber.

'Yes, I can't get over it,' said the young man. 'I just can't believe that I've done such a thing, because although I've always been in pain in my life, I'm not evil. I was just jealous and wanted Sandra to myself the way uncertain people do.'

'You're not charged with being evil,' Kleber said. 'A court doesn't take a state of mind into account, only the facts of the case. You're too young to know or remember, but during the last war millions of people were shot for a crime that they couldn't help: their crime was to exist.'

'You're not really a policeman, are you,' said the young man after holding his forehead in one hand for a long time, 'because I see we can talk together.'

'Well, I have ideas of justice,' said Kleber, 'that make me well loathed.'

'And do you care?'

'No,' said Kleber. 'The only trouble is that, like you, when I get a certain thing into my brain I also find the colours in a place artificial and too bright, and then it's goodbye to the rule-book.'

'What are we all going to do?' said the young man.

'I don't know,' said Kleber.

'What do you think justice is?' said the murdering bank clerk.

'It's certainly got nothing to do with just facts,' said Kleber.

'Is it to do with taking risks, walking the edge of precipices?'

'Much more likely. Especially if you're doing it for someone else.'

Yet Kleber knew he was lying, even though at the same time he was telling the truth. How, after all, do you tell a man, standing beside you and hit by a bullet, that he's dying?

6

While thinking of all this, Kleber got into the lift with three police clerks, each secure in her talent like news broadcasters, and each with her neat bundle of papers under her arm; the nightmare that she represented to Kleber was that they didn't know what a nightmare they and their papers meant.

'Which floor?' said one of them suspiciously, looking him up and down in his dirty street clothes.

'Fifth,' said Kleber. 'It's the one you get fired on, and pray God it never happens to you, or where would your boyfriends be?'

One of them sniggered; one of them had to do something.

'Stop making that sound,' said Kleber drily. 'It's a sign of mediocrity. I'd rather you picked your nose on the bus than that.'

'Are you really police?' said one of her friends in a voice of straightforward hatred.

'Yes,' said Kleber. 'You deal in paper, I deal in murder, but your crimes are the worst of all because they go unsigned.'

No one said a word in the lift after that, and no wonder—anyway, they had to get off at the fourth floor, the clerks' floor; they practically fled out of the lift. What Kleber was thinking was, how can you just leave a person or a place? Life was too breathless, too short; a swift, straight dash through terror, or so you hoped.

He got off at the fifth, where all the people who knew

everything lived, but even as Kleber walked down that clean corridor where everyone was a chief he was thinking: the position of a whole people can never be underrated, never be overstated. We move, he thought; we all still move and feel. He was walking down corridors past spotless rooms full of computer teams. Lean, eager little women with bad breath were earnestly pressing buttons and studying screens; it obviously wasn't any of their business to ask themselves why. He tried to remember back to when he had been so badly hurt in an affair that, at the time, he could think only of what pain meant; a sensation that was so immediate that it drove everything else out of him as imperiously as the blackness of death itself; he had been shot at from close quarters, in a room, by a man with a sawn-off twelve-bore, and he wondered why he had done such a stupid thing as try to capture the man, as a soldier might think in his last moment as he jumped the parapet at the front—why was I ever so stupid as to be sent into these bullets, though it was already too late to ask himself that question now. He stood and watched for a moment while small screens lit up with green writing, each set with the name of a Japanese firm on it, and thought: the style's gone, the class has gone, all gallantry's gone. What are the rest of us doing here? What a waste of public money, what a waste of people. I wanted justice when I joined the police, but all they do is hit, torture and record.

He went on down the straight corridor of that tangled concrete building until he reached Room 515, having taken in all he had ever seen with that third eye he had, until his mind bulged and other words, by compression, drove through his head. We can be taken, he thought, but not forced:

'Now we can state the prettiest cause of all,
How once heads wept and all men wept to see
That frightful dance of tears and death on wire,
The music of grief bursting from children's faces
Waiting beside the cold graves that killed us too
In cold fire;
But the graves were absent, the people in other
        places:
With the water from our eyes we paid their due.'

I must express it, thought Kleber; otherwise the dead
will go down as if they'd never lived. He didn't quite
know what the war was, being too young to have lived
through it; but what he did know was that the dead had
fought for a society for him, and what was happening to
that most expensive of all things was that it was being
wrecked and so what had they died for?

Oh, I definitely stand for the invisible, Kleber thought.
It'll be back; meantime I'll hold the fort the same way
they did. But it's now, he said, almost out loud. And now:

'Open a paper. You can see your eyes
In that mad, careful print accused.
What year? Which men? What cause?
Aren't we all times fused in pain?
Are we to do the self-same thing again?
Where are all my friends, my princes? What?
        All gone?
No pity here. Here, torture never ends.'

7

Kleber's chief's name was Verrières. Very, very few people had the nerve to call him Jean-Claude, and Kleber didn't even bother to. Kleber went into Room 515 and there was Verrières sitting behind his desk; the desk was like a country between them, or rather a country away from them.

'Ah, there you are,' said Verrières.

Mind, it was a nice desk. It had a nice ballpoint pen set on it, and a photograph of his wife, a thin, dull-looking little bat who looked as if she wouldn't mind a bit of torture being done in front of her when she wasn't too busy gossiping with the neighbours. Verrières, a fit, heavy man, sometimes enjoyed jumping on a prisoner in his liver across that desk. It was one way of getting someone to confess to something he mightn't have done as long as the duty officer was there to hold the suspect firmly down across the wood. Right now there was nothing but a brand-new blotter on the desk, brought out for show, with not a trace of ink on it, and another photograph on its left-hand side—Verrières' children, who had been trained, Kleber felt, to look as dull as the parents who had spat them out.

'All right,' said Verrières, 'don't bother to look where to sit down.'

'Don't worry,' said Kleber, 'I wasn't going to.'

Verrières breathed in heavily through his mouth and nose; he could afford to. After all, he was a police captain, and it was the kind of gesture he felt that he had to

41

make, the wages he drew. He said: 'Well, I'm afraid you know what this is about, Kleber.'

'Oh, yes, most certainly,' said Kleber. 'I'm not a new recruit.'

Verrières sucked at his teeth and brushed the spotted back of one enormous hand down the front of his nice coat, which hadn't a speck of anything on it except a minute hole in the lapel where the shop had taken the price tag off. 'What a cunt you really are, Kleber,' he said.

'Let's keep this calm, shall we?' said Kleber. 'Because after what's happened I've a feeling I'm going to be a private citizen again, and in that capacity you're in no position to lecture me, captain. So get on with it, because I feel like going out right now and having a beer. I've spent too long getting a dry throat talking to murderers, you know what I mean.'

'You having a go at me?'

'Not particularly,' said Kleber, 'but if I wanted to, why not? After all, you're the taxpayers' money.'

'You're not a bit afraid of me, are you?'

'Of course not,' said Kleber. 'Why should I be?'

'Lots of people are.'

'I know,' said Kleber, 'and I try to protect them from you.'

Now they were talking so equally that it was easy for Verrières to say: 'It's a good thing you're going to be sacked from the police, Kleber. Anyway, on the one hand. On the other it's a pity, because you were a good detective.'

'A bit too good for some people,' said Kleber.

'Me, you mean?'

'You've never done any detection in your life,' said Kleber. 'Your idea of a police investigation is just smacking people about, and quite frankly it doesn't work.'

Verrières sighed—after all, he didn't care what happened to Kleber one way or the other and he certainly wasn't going to be so stupid as to jump on Kleber, who was a good deal fitter and quicker than he was, and besides there wasn't any profit in Verrières doing such an energetic thing. Like most natural killers, he knew how to keep an even temper when it suited him. He said: 'You were insolent, independent.'

'I adore it when people talk about the living in the past tense,' said Kleber. 'It's like reading about your own death in the press.'

'Never mind that,' said Verrières on a note of false regret. 'What I will miss you for is you managed to get results.'

'I always get those,' said Kleber. 'Yes.'

'You hit that inspector much too hard,' said Verrières, taking a cigarette out of his side pocket, studying it and lighting it. He didn't offer Kleber one, knowing full well that Kleber would have refused it anyway. With Verrières, to lose face was almost as bad as to miss out on rank.

'He'd had his card well marked,' said Kleber. 'I'd told him clearly to stay right out of my cases.'

'He was newly promoted. He was raring to have a go.'

'I'm concerned with life and death,' said Kleber, 'not with the egos of newly promoted inspectors.'

'That's why you're going to be fired.'

'Yes,' said Kleber patiently, 'and that's why your inspector's in hospital with a broken nose. And you can be sure that a week or two in hospital will do him good; he'll be much easier going with whoever replaces me. He'll have had time to lie in bed and think about things.'

'You cheeky bastard,' said Verrières. 'All right—anyway, there's no point going on and on over this.'

'Nobody asked you to,' Kleber said.

'So you think you're going to get another job,' said Verrières, 'shrug all this off, just like that?'

'There's always the other side of the street,' said Kleber. 'And make a note of this, captain, it's the same street.'

The well-dressed bully opposite Kleber absorbed this, though it took him time. In the end he quoted the rule book, which was all he was empowered to do anyway once he was deprived of his pleasure in a situation. From the red fruitiness of its anticipation, Kleber having given it no chance, his fat face went puffy, white and flat, creased at the sides. He offered the flat of his huge hand at Kleber, but only in a symbolic way, then waved it as if by accident generally around his room. 'Well,' he said, 'you know what's going to happen now.'

'Certainly,' said Kleber. 'Here's my warrant card and here's my gun. Here's my driving licence; my car's outside. I'm still living my life, do you want that too? I'll give it to you with my identity card; tell me how far you want me to go.'

'Don't get hysterical.'

'Hard not to with people like you,' said Kleber. The night before he had dreamed again of his uncle, who had been killed in the war. His uncle's arm, that of a man whom as a child he had adored, was absolutely as firm around his as it had ever been, and he could feel the braid of the two gold rings that he had had as a reserve naval lieutenant, and he still believed, even in the daytime and even in front of Verrières, that it was all a matter of love. Kleber believed entirely that he was just standing in for the people he had loved who had disappeared but would presently come back again and discharge him from his agony of their absence.

'I'm going to have to put this to you formally,' said Verrières, 'because it's my job to. You're not fired; you're suspended. It'll be judged from inside the police, inside the mob, and it'll take a minimum of three months to sort out. You'll go up in front of one single high-ranking officer from the other side of the country who doesn't know any of us; he'll judge you when he's read all the papers, heard all the people in this, and there'll be no appeal.'

'I mightn't bother to wait for all that,' said Kleber. 'I might just resign and have done with it.'

'That's your choice, of course.'

'You bet it is,' said Kleber. 'I make the rules for me.'

'And that's always been your trouble. What are you trying to do? Commit suicide?'

'Depends on the fall.'

'Don't be so stupid,' said Verrières. 'Wait it out—you'll be doing everyone a favour, including yourself.'

'I'll be an ex-policeman on full wages until it comes up,' said Kleber. 'You know what that means? You call that a favour? What? The rest of the mob not even allowed to talk to me in the meantime?'

'I'm sorry to say that's part of it,' said Verrières with that look that the uninvolved always have. He picked up Kleber's gun off the desk and scooped it deftly, with his warrant card, into one of his drawers. He locked the drawer with a dry snapping sound and slipped the grim little key into his pocket.

'Don't try to impress me so hard,' said Kleber; 'you're ruining your make-up.'

'Out you go,' said Verrières. 'We're finished with you for the moment. You'll be told when we want you; don't bother to ring.'

'I'm not likely to.'

'Buy yourself a beer, go down into the street.'

'It's where I usually live.'

'Go into a bar, get a beer, get pissed, get lost; have fun on the taxpayer.'

'OK,' said Kleber.

'The pity of it was,' said Verrières, yawning, 'as I say, that you were quite a good detective.'

'I agree with you,' said Kleber, leaving. 'Anyway, I was a fucking sight better at it than you are, so think about that.'

It was odd being fired, whether you were prepared for it or not. Kleber left the room on the note he wanted, turning on his heel with all the contempt he had in him, and walked downstairs. Immediately he was thinking of Elenya. He thought, at least I've got you, darling. He still felt glad that he had hit the inspector, who had been a low-ranking, bad copy of Verrières. What did any of it matter, after all? Now at least he could really concentrate on Elenya, on their joint lives.

Outside in the street it was pouring with rain that wept from a huge purple cloud that lay above Sébastopol, and he turned his coat collar up against it.

Tomorrow was his birthday. He and Elenya were going to make a feast of it; they'd decided that long in advance. He was sorry they couldn't have a child together, but because of what had happened to her in the past that unfortunately wasn't possible. But was that really so important, he wondered as he made for the Métro, as long as they'd got each other?

The trains rushed out of the tunnels and stopped against the platforms with hissing brakes, and Kleber, waiting for the doors to open, was suffused with a great feeling of love for his wife that he felt there was no way and no need to explain.

*

Mortal pain and great evil were both well armed, but he knew that. Why they were all there to face such final, vital matters was a different question and, as usual, there was no time in his head for him to debate it now that he was going home to his wife.

But as he changed trains at Châtelet a little cunt came up to Kleber and gave him a big slap on the back, a slap much too hard for friendship. 'Well,' said this little idiot, 'how are things in the police today? Making plenty of arrests, are we?'

'Don't mess around with me today,' said Kleber. 'I'll forgive you the smack on the back this once, but the silly jokes… it isn't the right time, the right day.'

'Don't be so stupid,' said the vexing little man, taking another slap at Kleber. 'The way we live, news travels fast where you're concerned, and I hear you've got problems.'

'They happen to all of us.'

'Maybe they do,' said the agile little man, circling around Kleber, 'but to be in the police yet no longer belong to it—I find that really artful as a problem, almost artistic, baby.' He had a mat on his chest and was naked under a pair of worn overalls. Kleber had done him twice for thieving, and now he stood stock still in the tunnel, which rang under their feet, and considered him seriously while the last of the bank clerks scurried by, looking at their Japanese watches. He smacked Kleber on the arm and trod on his foot as if by accident.

'Look, fuck off,' said Kleber. 'I'm not asking for the moon; you've probably already stolen it. I honestly don't want to have anything to do with you. I don't want to have to get heavy. I'm in love with my wife and tomorrow it's my birthday, so I'm full of goodwill to all men, but if you don't get lost straight away, sweetheart, I might suddenly change my mind. Are you reading me?'

'Nobody needs to read you any more,' said the man, giving Kleber another of his smacks, 'you're finished.'

'No,' said Kleber, 'that's the part you've got wrong, darling.' He hit him really hard exactly where the other man didn't want it, i.e. in the liver. It was a terrible blow, number four after the killing one (head, heart, balls, liver), and the poor sod doubled over like a tent in a gale, stricken, and fell down slap on the concrete. After he had done it, Kleber fished him upright. 'I'm like most people,' he said. 'I really do hate being fucked about by silly little cunts.' His victim had sicked up a little blood against the Métro tiles; Kleber looked at it in a professional way and decided that it wasn't serious blood. He had seen plenty of serious blood, the fatal kind, with or without bubbles in it; in his job he had seen too much death and blood altogether. There was a bar he had been paid to know at Châtelet, and Kleber half-helped, half-dragged his victim up to it—it was a bar where the law were found at one end of the counter, and the villains, pimps and con men at the other. He shoved his individual through the door of the place into the bright light and said loudly to the general assembly: 'A friend of yours, not one of mine, so take care of him.' Nobody said or did anything except stare at them, so Kleber threw his man at an empty bench, went to the bar and ordered a kir. 'I'm warning you not to do what he just did,' he said in a conversational tone, 'all right? There's your proof.'

Somebody coughed at the police end; otherwise there was a short silence in the place, which was mauve with smoke. Kleber didn't care. He just leaned against the bar on his right elbow, looking abstractedly into his drink, his face arranged in a white, triangular manner, although every time a word was spoken around him he looked at the speaker directly, analysing every movement and glance, his eyes going darker by a shade and examining sideways but unwavering, the way eyes do when they depend on the wits behind them for a living.

Kleber was no middle-class detective but a street man, and everybody in that bar, no matter what they were or what they did for a living, knew it. The only armchair he could remember was the one he had once been tortured in because of a case that had got into a terrible muddle when he had been young. Kleber never solved his cases in armchairs; if there was one thing he hated more than armchairs, it was the people who sat in them. True misery lived in the streets, and that was where Kleber was used to dealing with it; rich suicides, as far as he was concerned, could wait until afterwards, a long time afterwards. The object of existence (if indeed there was any) had gradually become apparent to him: it was of course to become the other—if not, what further point could there be in anything so absurd? He decided that sin had slipped into himself and everyone else through necessity—in Kleber's world it was much better to lose your soul than not eat. Invisible things like a soul could always be found again, but in a city food was a much more serious problem, and he saw it in men's faces everywhere he looked.

The man Kleber had hit sprawled, dazed, his eyes crossed, with some brand-new pink blood on his lips, exactly where he had been thrown, like a half-empty sack of something, which embarrassed the off-duty police having drinks at their end. It upset the barmen too—not that they were stupid enough to do anything about it. The coppers, all of whom he had known for at least fifteen years and worked with, turned their backs ostentatiously on Kleber when they saw him come in and created very loud and pointless conversation that they would never have dreamed of otherwise; it was banal even for them. It amused Kleber.

'As I was saying to the old woman—'

'Yes, Marie's the same.'

'They're all the bloody same. Women—'

'I reckon my kids are old enough to go down to the Tarn for the summer on their own now. I've hired them horses and canoes.'

'Why don't the six of us all spend August together if we can get the dates to fit?'

'August? You might as well be talking about paradise. It's nearly a year away.'

'That bloke in the corner there looks a bit sick.'

'What bloke? You haven't seen anyone, new boy, and don't be a cunt or you'll be back on the beat.'

'There's this disco called the Galaxy which is literally crawling with birds. Françoise found me with one in the hedge last summer. God, she was choked. I thought, oh, well, that's it, then. But she sort of recovered after a couple of weeks.'

'They have to get over it really, the poor cows. Which of you male chauvinist pigs is buying another round?'

Behind their broad, stupid, obedient backs Kleber laughed out loud and ordered another kir. He was quite alone at the centre of the bar, got served last, and reluctantly at that—the barmen knew their part all right, though God knows, Kleber said aloud, their lines aren't exactly difficult ('I'd kill myself if I were you, and do it quickly too'). Looking at them, he found he couldn't help it, but he was enjoying himself. He thought he would stay on in the bar for a while longer to see what would happen—at the same time he daydreamed about Elenya: they were walking hand in hand in some city.

Every door there was open to them both and hundreds of people were leaning out of their windows, smiling and waving to them and calling for them to come into their houses.

Kleber waited. He knew what was going to happen next, and he watched it lumber up to him through a gaze which had abruptly narrowed. He focused on six of them, all from the villains' end of the bar, all heavy, all alike. He found himself supposing something that he had never dreamed that he could suppose—that Poland now, anyway to him, had become a mythical land whose past, having entirely been paid for over and over, had now been cast off like a filthy old coat so that everyone inside those new frontiers was standing about, upright; everyone there was pale and young. Everyone was waiting for them both, reaching their strong hands out to them. Elenya called out happily: 'We're just coming…!'

'How's everything going, Kleber?' said the first thief.

'That's the question you ought to be trying to answer,' said Kleber, indicating the motionless figure on the bench with his head.

'We hear you're in a bit of bother.'

'I'm not,' said Kleber. 'But you are, or very shortly will be.'

'What bother's that, then?'

'It's called an ambulance,' said Kleber. 'As you're illiterate I'll let you into a secret: you spell it with an A. It takes you to a place called a hospital—you spell that with an H—and with any luck it'll all be a one-way ticket.'

'I love it when busted coppers try to come on strong,' said a man in a lightweight check suit. He brightened his right fist up with his other hand; it was the only cleaning job he knew.

Another of them tipped his beer over Kleber. 'Christ,' said this man, overflowing with his own laughter, 'why, I must be going blind or something to waste my drink on some cunt like that.'

'I could help you along with going blind if you like,' said Kleber, 'but I shouldn't encourage me.'

'Thank Christ nobody is you,' said the knuckle-polisher, 'you horrible individual.'

'So you've been busted, Kleber.'

'Yes,' said Kleber. 'And what that means to you is that I've thrown the rule book away, so I should be very careful indeed if I were you.'

'Oh, I love it when the law gives you a chance like that,' said one of them. He trod on Kleber's feet. 'Your shoes need cleaning,' he said coldly. 'So why don't you get down on your knees and spit on them? No, wait, I'll do it for you'—and he spat on Kleber's legs.

'Is there going to be any trouble here?' said a barman, leaning across the counter.

'I should think it's highly likely,' said Kleber, 'so I should get well hidden before it starts.'

'I just don't want any trouble.'

'Then change your customers,' said Kleber. 'If you get rid of the law you'll get rid of the villains, and then this place will seem almost like normal. Then you'll be able to call it the Policemen's Arms and practically get away with it.'

The barman, who was rather new to the atmosphere of the place, understood that all right and abruptly vanished. None of the police at the other end took any notice of what was going on. They were still talking about next year's holidays. Or last year's.

'I love you for what you are!' Kleber shouted to them.

'What it is to have friends, I must say!' He picked up his kir, but one of his men gave his arm a sharp jog, so that Kleber's drink went all over him. Kleber put his empty glass in that man's side pocket and smashed it there with the flat of his hand. The man shrieked a little as the glass went into him and Kleber said kindly: 'Don't do things like that, darling. Not when you're with the grown-ups.' He added: 'Why don't you go off and powder your nose? You're beginning to bleed a little here and there, did you know?'

'Oh, I say,' said the man in the check suit, 'I think we ought to get this big upstanding police officer another drink, don't you?' He said to the barman: 'Serve us a big kir, cuntie, and do it fast.'

'Yes,' said the barman, who suddenly found he was doing everything rather faster than he was used to, but before he could get the stuff out of the bottle and into the glass a young joker in a smart yellow coat came up half-pissed and wrung Kleber by the hand. He turned this friendly gesture into extreme effort, and did his best to break Kleber's wrist. 'Oh, so sorry,' he smirked. 'Did that hurt?'

'Nothing like as much as this is going to,' said Kleber. With an apparently meaningless movement he took the man by one finger and deftly broke it.

'Ah! Ah!' the man shouted from inside his yellow coat, wringing himself by his finger.

'I know why you wanted to shake hands with me,' said Kleber genially. 'It was for the five years' sunshine I bought your brother last year—he wanted you to remind me how much he's been enjoying himself down by the sea in Fresnes: tell him I'll do it for him again the minute he comes out. Any time.' He added seriously to the man with the broken finger: 'I should get that seen to straight away if I were you. It's broken in two places, and it'll never heal properly again if you don't. However, it's your finger, not mine. And as for your brother in Fresnes, next time he comes out of the shadows tell him not to go around any more screwing old ladies and ripping them off for their savings. It'll save what's left of the human race a lot of work.' The man stood among them sobbing and sucking at his broken finger and Kleber said: 'Don't cry. Your victims can do that for you, can't they?' He said to the other villains in a general, conversational tone: 'Look how silly it is, won't you? Smashing a man's finger just to give the doctors more work.'

'It could be your turn next,' said one of them, but he was standing well back.

'All right,' said Kleber. 'Well, come on then. Who's next, shithead?'

Just then a man came into the place whom Kleber had had his eye on for a very long time. All the law got up as he arrived and left in a body, and Kleber knew why: they had been paid. The new man came up to the bar, looked around the scene that his presence was emptying and said to the little mob: 'You lot, fuck off, at once.'

They did it, all right; they were thankful to melt away from him. He looked at the corpse-like figure that Kleber had deposited at the table at the back and said: 'Was that you who hurt him?'

'You bet it was,' said Kleber. 'Apart from his head, what else is wrong with him?'

'Well, fancy,' said the man. 'For once you could be making a very serious error yourself. I'm just waiting for it.' Kleber hated the man. He was very high up in drugs, fine, OK, but it wasn't that. He had tried to kill Mark once, who never hit anything harder than a bank, and had only just missed.

'I love your elegant conversation,' the man said.

'I'm not surprised,' said Kleber. 'It's the same way I love corruption. Everyone who knows me knows that. It's just they need to be more careful. Mind, as you know, I warn people first, but it's also the last time.'

'You'll never get back into the police,' said the man, 'the word on you's gone all around. You're fucked, you realise that.'

'You haven't many friends either,' Kleber said.

'I hardly need them in my position, do I?' said the man. He drew off a yellow pigskin glove to reveal some nasty-looking white fingers, which he used to screw an American cigarette into a holder and then light with a gold lighter.

'I should look out if I were you,' said Kleber. 'So far you've only bought the police, and that doesn't include me any more.'

'I'm truly sorry for you,' said the man. They stood up to each other like mortal boxers.

'You be sorry for yourself,' Kleber said, 'if you know what the word means.'

'Are you asking for more trouble?' said the man incredulously.

'Certainly,' said Kleber. 'I take the stuff in any quantity at all from funny little folk like you.'

'You might just be singing a very unhappy song,' the man said.

'Let's see who's alive to sing the chorus,' said Kleber. 'What do you think? They could be saying amen over you while I'm sunning myself in my garden. With my wife.'

'You're walking very, very near the edge,' the man said. 'You really ought to start taking good care of yourself in your position.'

'I don't know much about positions,' said Kleber, 'but while we're talking of them your arse is flying in the fucking wind, so look out. You touch my wife, make the faintest contact, one sneer, one phone call, even a smile from your rotten face from the far corner of a bar and you'll get a pauper's funeral, I'll see to it. Now get out of my sight, cunt.'

'You're making a very big mistake.'

'That's what you call it, you ignorant bastard,' said Kleber. 'I call it minding my own business, and all you need worry about is that I don't start minding yours— you won't have any business left if I do, you understand?'

'I mean to run this part of the city, Kleber,' the man said. 'Run it on snow.'

'I realise that,' said Kleber, 'but just make sure that you never trouble me or my friends, because if ever you do you won't know where, you won't know when, but you'll fucking know why.'

'There mightn't be room for both of us,' the man said. 'The whole place mightn't be big enough.'

'This bar's big enough for me right now,' said Kleber, 'especially without you in it. Now get lost. Bye-bye, sweetheart.'

8

Kleber realised all at once that he was a pretty sick man. He was sick from his dreams. Only the other night he had had one. In it he was close to death. In the strange atmosphere where he found himself he could practically reach out and touch death and this time he did so. Compared with life it was the wrong side of the coin, the side you lost on when you bet on it. Death was because of what had happened to everyone in his world. It was a little world really, but it wouldn't have made any difference if it had been a big one; the suffering was the same. Death appeared as a dark, colossal building with no style that soared above him with its dark walls. It was partly so dark because it was as neutral as an office block. But there was more involved than that, because God only knew what there was inside it. Kleber in his frightful sleep hoped there was nothing, but how could he possibly know? The place had thousands of windows, but they were all silent, black and blind. Because he was there looking at it it scrutinised him back, as it would, he knew, anyone else who happened to pass; it wasn't anything you could get past. Also, he noticed that there was no door into it. Of course, he wondered who had built such a horrible thing and why, for there was nothing to be seen inside that block, nor means even of seeing anything. But instinct told him that there was very probably something that could see him. The place was as cold and ancient as a destination from which you couldn't return, yet it was as new to Kleber as yesterday's concrete. Presently he heard himself turn in his bed and woke up sweating with terror from what he had seen. He felt ready to turn to any influence, literally anything at all that could help him with it.

The spectre of illness plagued him too, and he knew that it would come to him when his body wore out, and he often prayed that he would be helped through it if ever he lived long enough for it to come and threaten him. Indeed, he had been in the front line for so long now, relief never coming, that he expected all risks to come to him as a long-serving soldier would and was really quite glad of his situation and of what he was doing in a curious way, though he couldn't honestly have said why. He couldn't even have told Elenya why, though there were times when he would have given anything he possessed on earth to have spoken to her absolutely, and told her absolutely why, but so beautiful a reaction to life would have been completely illogical, sentimental, ridiculous and absurd, and Kleber knew that all too well; for the simplest things were also always the hardest, and that was the first thing he had ever learned in the street.

But he was tired of living on the edge of the precipice he had searched for, and hoped desperately at night that somebody would come.

Oh, restless and uneasy spirit, trying to do the whole work of the world for it, only he saw it as his role, as far as he could see, and as far as he knew how to know anyway.

'As long as I don't suffer too much when it comes to it,' he said to himself, 'I can manage the rest; after all, everyone else has to.'

It's strange how terrible the world can be when you get the feeling that you might be coming to the end of it. The planet itself may be round all right, but men like

Kleber, right or wrong, had to go in a straight line: it was the kind of line that a knife makes across a throat, a very sharp knife. Yet other people had been killed by the bloody thing, far too many of them, in stupid, pointless ways, sent off to the other world by mediocre people who didn't know what a risk meant, and Kleber couldn't see what, compared with them, made him so fucking special.

Kleber made a phone call to his wife.

'Is that you, Kleber? Where are you, darling?'

'Some stupid bar in the second arrondissement. I'm afraid I'm going to be late.'

'Yes, but remember it's your birthday tomorrow, and we've made plans.'

'As if I could forget.' He said suddenly: 'I adore you, Elenya; always remember that.'

'I know,' she said. 'Why, what's wrong? Is something the matter with you?'

'No, I just felt that I had to say it.'

'Why? I know it well, in every way.'

'Hundreds of reasons in my head that I can't explain. Just love.'

'Then come back and capture me the minute you can,' she said swiftly. 'How did things go at work, by the way? Over that man you hit?'

'Oh, well, you know how it is,' said Kleber. 'What had to happen did happen and I've been suspended, but you don't need to worry. Meantime I think I've got to go and see a man.'

'Mark?'

'How did you guess?'

'Is he in trouble?'

'I think he soon will be, because I've just had a silly conversation with someone, but I'll explain when I get back.'

'Who'd be married to a copper?'

'Being married to an ex-copper's even worse.'

'You make a better hero with no gun.'

'I'm glad I got rid of the thing,' said Kleber. 'I hate them.'

'What about supper, then?'

'Leave me something cold if you like. I'll be back in the night. I don't know when.'

'You never do, and it never matters.'

'I don't care whether the food's hot or cold,' said Kleber, 'as long as you're there to go with it.'

'You know I always shall be.'

'Christ, my wonderful luck to have you, darling,' said Kleber. 'I'll never know why I've been so lucky. What's that music I can hear in the background? Radio Warsaw?'

'Yes, as usual. I'm afraid there's been more trouble there.'

'Try not to worry too much, and I love you.'

'I love you too.'

'Bye-bye for now, my darling.'

'Bye.'

E-major was a terrible key, the key that the signature tune of Radio Warsaw was in, thought Kleber. There were too many black notes in it, reminding him of what had started to go dark in man as the result of a cross that was too heavy to bear. In Elenya's country clouds had come to obscure the sun just when they should not, and the trouble that had come there was just the trouble that must never come, blocking and rotting people, destroying their hope and pride while the strong were asleep or dead or boasting, but mostly dead. Elenya had once, but only once, told him that at times in her sleep she could still somehow, because she was much too young to know, hear them screaming as they died in '39. It wasn't a period you made any great effort to forgive, and above all not in Kleber's case. He shook his head as he went back to the bar and sat down. He shook it in sadness because he knew the hard work that had given him his living would one day take it away again. He didn't really mind in one way; so many excellent people having gone the same road in front of him, and so many crowding with him behind. But the whole experience carried its own sadness in it all the same. He felt so old in his mind, yet he was only forty, so he wondered why he was laden down by sorrow.

'I don't know,' Kleber muttered, 'but I feel uneasy for Elenya and must be on guard for her day and night, every second of the day and night; instinct's its own prayer.'

And yet, as Kleber was aware, to everything that lives on earth everything and anything can happen, and not only that but still worse—finality can happen, and happen suddenly too.

So he went out into the street. The rain had temporarily stopped and although it was still deep winter the sky had by some miracle cleared so that a number of stars could be seen, and Kleber, looking up, thought for a moment that no sky above any such great city had ever been so beautiful, although, of course, it was bloody cold. Presently he went down Sébastopol to the Bar Tahiti, where he knew he would find Mark. He had to find Mark. After what he had just heard he knew he had to find Mark at once.

Mark was in the middle of dinner when Kleber

arrived; the Tahiti had a nice little Vietnamese kitchen going at the back of the place, and you could eat European food there too if you wanted. Mark and Kleber generally mixed them.

Mark said to Kleber: 'Sit down. Eat. Let's start dinner all over again. Christ, for a busted copper you've arrived at exactly the right time. You're just the man I need to talk to. Are you always as sharp on time as this?'

'Usually,' said Kleber. 'I mightn't be alive if I weren't.' He pulled a chair away from a neighbouring table and sat down. He added: 'I've been looking for you too.'

'It's like some fucking love affair.'

'Well, it's been going on long enough for us to get married if you looked at it that way,' said Kleber, 'and, who knows, we might need to get each other out of trouble.'

'I know *you're* in it, all right,' said Mark, 'but what's my problem?'

'Yours is a problem that wears yellow pigskin gloves and does things to girls he'd better give up if he wants to stay on in life—I'll put it that way.'

'Ah,' said Mark. 'Ah, that's worked up, has it?'

'If he could borrow a chainsaw he'd fell you like a tree.'

'I know the cure for a chainsaw,' Mark said. 'You encourage it to cut into something that looks like wood only it isn't, and by the time it's burned itself out it's cheaper to buy a new one.'

Mark didn't say anything more for a while. He sat with his gaze dawdling over the tablecloth and reached out abstractedly for the bottle in the ice-bucket and poured himself a glass of wine. This he turned around on the pretty linen tablecloth, staring into it, and said without looking at Kleber: 'What a pity it is that neither of us are very nice men.'

'Oh, come on,' said Kleber. 'Who needs nice men when you can get straightforward ones?'

'It would have been something to be nice, though. You know, kind, a good husband, a good father.'

'That got killed off in the war,' said Kleber, 'all that—it must have been, because where do you find it?'

'It's somewhere in my heart,' Mark said. 'I can feel it in there somewhere; it's getting at it that's the problem. I tell you, I wouldn't mind giving up the life I lead, you know, marry a good woman, buy a house in the country if there are any left, settle down.'

'You'd buy four houses,' said Kleber, 'marry three women, never settle down. I know you.'

'It would have been nice, though,' Mark said.

'It must have been the war, I tell you,' said Kleber. 'I tell you it's no use trying to get the violence out of us now. You know that. What's the matter with you? Are you ill or something?'

'Ill? I'm never ill. But I mightn't have very long to live. You just marked my card.'

'I hate that man,' said Kleber.

'OK, then. I need a hand. Will you give me a hand?'

'You mean a bodyguard?'

'The bastard's trying to tumble me,' said Mark slowly, 'and, yes, I need you tonight.'

'OK,' said Kleber. 'I didn't say I wouldn't do it, did I?'

'Try some of this veal,' said Mark. 'It's excellent. Yes, you know these wicked little wars that go on around here.'

'I certainly should do—who better?'

'Try some of this too for an evening's work,' said Mark, passing him an envelope. 'It's delicious. It tastes of money: ten thousand English pounds' worth.'

'It's a taste I don't greatly care for,' said Kleber. 'I don't need it that much.'

'I agree it's an acquired taste,' said Mark, 'but you'll get used to it, like everyone else. Now just take it and don't fuck me about.'

'We'll go to the races on it together, the two of us,' said Kleber. 'Elenya's a wonderful girl for spotting a winner.' He put the envelope carefully in the pocket he didn't spend from. 'All right, give me a little map of what we're into.'

'There's a place called the Twelve Bar, Rue St-Denis.'

'I know it; who doesn't? What's the name of the man who runs it? That's right, they call him the Count of Madrid.'

'I'm supposed to pick up a lot of money there this evening, but I don't like it. I think it's a trap.'

'I see,' said Kleber. 'The only trouble is I've got no gun.' Each knew what the other meant: a man's best appearance on any stage is usually his last, but neither of them said so. Instead, they talked of practical, immediate matters.

'Don't give a fuck about the gun,' said Mark. 'Right outside in the street you'll find a red 604. Here are the keys.'

'I'll go in front,' said Kleber; 'you follow. They won't get you tonight or any night.'

'That's it,' said Mark. 'As for the gun, you'll find a nine-millimetre pistol in the glove compartment.'

'That's a fine weapon.'

'You can trust it,' said Mark. 'I loaded it myself, and there's a spare magazine with it. Now I want you to see my car. It's a bright blue CX, and I'll be thirty yards behind you all the time.'

'Just stick to me like shit to a blanket,' said Kleber, 'and everything'll be OK, you'll see. What's the pistol?'

'Browning.'

'Oh, I like those pistols a lot,' said Kleber. 'I've had lots of practice with them.'

'Now be careful if I'm right and it's a trap,' said Mark. 'I'm as frightened for your life as I am for mine.'

Kleber shook his head. 'Don't be. You're preaching to the converted. I haven't done twenty-two years in the police for nothing, and, as for being careful, it's always been my trade to be careful.'

'That's it, then,' said Mark. He got up and put money on the table. 'Sorry to have kept you,' he said to the waiter, 'but we had a lot to talk about.'

'I think I know your friend, don't I?'

'You don't know anything or anyone,' Mark said, 'not if you know what's good for you. That's why I left a heavy tip, darling.'

What a filthy business killing is, thought Kleber. It would be the fifth time round for him if he had to do it again. He got into the Peugeot and started it. He found the gun OK, checked it with his hands in the darkness of the car while the motor idled; then, happy with it, laid it on the seat beside him. Please God, he said to himself out loud, don't let me have to do any killing. He just hoped Mark had made a mistake about a trap and that no one would be waiting for them, because he didn't want to blow any heads off. He thought of random things while he waited for Mark to pull out behind him, such as why life had to be so bloody bitter for some people—mind, he had had a good dinner, got his money and was doing it for his mate. Even so he couldn't forget, because of having been in the police for so long, how tragically small the corpse of a man looked—couldn't get it out of his mind as he put the car in gear. Through grief for the rottenness of what society had become, through grief as you mourn over the body of a woman you once loved. Kleber thought some more as he watched Mark follow him in his mirror—how, when you were struck by a nine-millimetre bullet, it wasn't a bit like in the cinema where you slowly fell and agonised as you spoke the hero's last lines: it was the same as being hit with a sledgehammer; it was a blow that sent you across the length of a room; it was like being hit by a lorry. Again and again Kleber found himself asking just what a human life, any life, was really worth.

As for his own death, he didn't know, as these horrible images scampered through his brain, whether he was afraid of it or not, and that worried him, because he knew that his ignorance of his own end meant that he had understood no one else's.

What was the use of dismissing metaphysics if you didn't even know what the term meant? Murdered people, murdered countries—Kleber wondered uneasily what he had done, what he was guilty of even to be in a position to set himself such a question. But what he did know was that it had been done and that he had been responsible for some part of it, and that there was no conceivable answer to the past, to what had passed. No.

I do my own things best, thought Kleber, for the excellent reason that there's no one but myself to challenge them; I'm on my own. You would do it, you insisted on it. But what did it all come back to? Always the same point: 'What's a dead person worth? A poisoned, murdered person? A dead old woman or, worse still, a young one.' And now he was beginning to realise what a solitary figure he had become—not through lack of warmth but opportunity and occasion: he had always taken such pride in a foolish thing called managing to cope on one's own, entirely on one's own. It had got him into police work and he knew now, for the first time, that he would never get out of it as long as he had flesh on his arms; even if he was no longer in the police the habit of investigation in some form would remain with him for as long as he lived.

Kleber put his wipers on because there was still that eternal driving rain; he had the lights of Mark's CX directly behind him in his mirror. But he found he was feeling and thinking only about Elenya—it was strange the things you found yourself thinking about when you were in a tight, difficult situation, for simultaneously he was back at school, doing English; he was back in some half-forgotten day in a half-forgotten classroom with flies buzzing under the lights and he was copying out lines for the big exam. As a huge love for his wife rushed into him while he drove east up Sébastopol for no reason he knew of he remembered:

> 'He cast his eye upon Emelya,
> And therewithal he bleynte and cried Ah!
> As though he stongen were unto the herte.'

And so the year 1400 placed its hand on Kleber; he was fifteen as well as forty while he drove the Peugeot fast up the boulevard. He felt his wife in his blood as he changed gear for the lights, her mind in his eyes, but above all her flat warm Polish hand in his. Yet at the same time, on another level there was that old woman of eighty-six whom he had had to see die in front of him on a wet bed in a naked flat, murmuring as she sank: 'Oh, dear. Oh, dear. Oh, dear. How long? How long? How long?'

She had been knocked down by a mad young thief, whitish, who had broken in, against a grandfather clock she had with a picture of Windsor Castle on its face that she had inherited from a British relation, and Kleber had been called in, but he could get no meaning out of her and had just had to wait until the ambulance came for her while he minded her broken ribs as best he could. So love and hatred, life and death, rain, sun and the will of man, all the vast highways and crossroads of existence entailed a great danger for Kleber, the risk along the edge of the precipice that he found he had to run and was this minute running; it seemed that it was only by looking into the abyss that was constantly beside him that he could know what living was; and that only as death, its very opposite, kept trying to crowd in on him.

As he drove he remembered with some kind of a smile how he had passed the English exam without any difficulty; there had been no more to it than pushing open a door that wasn't even locked. Of course, he had done the work involved. But why? he wondered now. Why had it been necessary for him to be anything but so complex as an intelligent man to get through so stupid an experience as his own birth and death when ruthless and selfish people made such a spectacularly simple job of it? He thought that it was a bloody good thing that the devil never appeared in daylight; God help us poor feeble people if he ever did. He thought what a pleasant kind of life it would be if you never had to run a risk of any kind but just go on through life until you somehow wore out, watching the sun wearing its way around the earth from a soft chair with a drink handy. His dreams had recently been a warning for his fears, but he had not been able to obey their signs, and so found himself in the 604 this night; he had been too busy to

68

have any time to heed any warnings today.

He was remembering vaguely, for some reason, a case he had dealt with where a man had written his girlfriend a nice letter after they had split up on thick notepaper which he had headed 'Requiem' in beautiful handwriting, and then killed himself.

Then everything happened. He had his hand on the gun where it lay on the seat beside him all through the ride and he was going up the narrow street with Mark behind him when a rusty old Estaffette crossed him to block the road, but Kleber was out of the Peugeot and out on the pavement before it had stopped, with his gun searching fatally at the first of the four men who had spilled out of the van, men who were already pumping lead out of sawn-off twelve-bores into his now-empty, still gently rolling car. Kleber, already hidden behind a parked motor, picked the first one off as the Peugeot rolled slowly but heavily into the van. The poor bastards had no time to find out where on earth these mortal bullets were coming from, and they literally sprang into death as they fired in the wrong direction—Kleber was much too fast for them; he wasn't a street-trained copper for nothing. They flung themselves in a terrible, awkward dance across the street, into death under the impact of Kleber's lead, three of them. To Kleber it all seemed like slow motion—tragedy slowed down into fire, movement and noise; other traffic behind the two vehicles hooted impatiently at the delay, having no idea what was going on. Kleber felt there was something wrong about it as he fired; it was like picking off chickens in a farmyard, it was all so easy, too easy, they never had a chance. All Kleber had to do was steady the pistol, aim and squeeze, and it was all over in thirty seconds. Over for them, but not for him; he knew he had to live on. Even as he fired at the third wretched idiot he found that he was asking himself the central question—what was the value of the life he was taking? A lot? A little? Nothing at all?—as the now-dead body smashed its way across the street into the side of the van. The fourth man leaped into it, rocking off in reverse across the pavement, turned and fucked off. Kleber fired one into his back tyre and was satisfied to see it go down, the smart pace drifting into a crooked lopsided limp—the wheel rim screamed as it hit some cement, gave off a stinking smoke and vanished around a corner. Kleber stood there with the Browning in his hand and looked at the three men he had shot, their bodies lying anyhow in a horrid flat pattern on the street, because the last dance you did was on your back. The Peugeot sat there smoking, its windows smashed by shotgun fire.

He stuck the pistol away in his waistband and walked swiftly towards Mark's CX; he was rolling up to meet him, the passenger door already open. Kleber got in and crashed his door shut and they started to move fast.

'I shan't have any more trouble from them,' Mark said.

'I'm afraid you will; the chief got away.'

'He won't last long now.'

'I hope not.'

'I'll deal with it.'

'Deal with it hard,' said Kleber; 'you'll never get a second chance.' He was remembering a time in his childhood when a peasant friend of his had suddenly seen a snake in their path and instantly cut it in two with his spade.

'Never mind,' said Mark. 'You did that bloody well.'

They left the scene exactly as it was, backed up the CX, sped off up a side-street and disappeared just as people were beginning to sneak out of their houses to see what had happened and alert the police.

What was that song he had once heard an Australian sing in a bar?

> 'Ride hard, ride hard.
> I'm a most indifferent guy,
> And it's a most important day.
> Ride hard, ride hard,
> Until the dawn of day.'

But it was only slowly that you began to understand what it meant.

There was another terrible time when a murderer said to Kleber: 'I'll survive, you know.'

'To do what?'

'I'll bring the moonlight down on his head.'

'What does that mean?'

'What do you think it means?' the man said. 'It's a light that's white, cold and fatal.'

'Death?'

'What else could it be?' said the man, staring terribly at the wall past Kleber's head. 'He wore glasses, but that won't save his fucking sight, I'll see to it.'

The language of the street.

Mark dropped Kleber off by his own car. The two men shook hands and Mark said: 'Thanks. Go home, rest, read, make love, relax. There won't be any noise about this, I'll see to it. You've saved me. I'll ring you tomorrow; goodnight, Kleber, my friend.'

'It's my birthday tomorrow. You remember?'

'How many? Forty-four?'

'Don't you remember how we used to celebrate them?

I'm sorry the head man got away.'

'Ah, but that's war for you in this city,' Mark said. 'It can't be helped.'

'I hadn't time for all four of them.'

'Don't you worry,' Mark said. 'We'll see to him together. Right now you go home and get your rest.' And he got in his car and left.

Standing by his own motor, Kleber, for some reason or none, remembered how he had recently dreamed of death. The event had appeared to him as a fragile, wizened shape, dark, neither man nor woman; there were shreds of white hair clinging to its head. It smiled a smile that was really no smile, revealing black gaps in its mouth and, since it couldn't speak, it made terrible whining noises at him somewhere between tears and sniggers. That was one of the most sinister nightmares he had ever had. He was also reminded, as he got into his car and started it, of a tramp he had once seen pushing an old pram full of rubbish and empty bottles across a sunny square.

He looked at his watch and found it was a quarter to three in the morning of his birthday, October the fourth, and so he drove home as quickly as he could with those three deaths behind him to be back with Elenya at last.

But driving back in a stunned manner after what he had just done on the street, he found that what he mainly thought about was modern art, and that great painter, Sickert, who had presented to him the black, bruised faces of prostitutes, their eyes for ever shaded and looking sideways away from life under their cheap hats. The artist, as artists must, had captured that suffering and intelligence beyond their wounds, behind their darkened eyes, the mouths half-smiling for their trade, and the stained cheeks of disease under their rouge. Beautiful and doomed, they stood for Kleber—he felt he almost was them. Wars are easier forgotten than fought, but courage is always courage, and Kleber always admired that. If you knocked out individual courage, he thought, people capable of fighting on their own, it was a whole society that dimmed, went dark, was switched out, and he was determined to keep what had been battled for bright and alive, well lit, funny, with that brilliance that the dead would have appreciated if only they hadn't died for it so that civilisation should stay alive.

9

He got back to the ground-floor flat they had and he was so glad to get in and hear her call out: 'Is that you, Kleber?'

'Yes, here I am at last,' he said, taking her in his arms. 'Sorry to have been so long. I couldn't help it.'

'Happy birthday, my darling,' she said, kissing him, after which she held him back from her and looked at the face she had just kissed and said anxiously: 'Are you all right?'

'It's been a busy evening,' he said. 'The less you know of it the better.'

'You always know what you're doing,' she said, 'so I just let you get on with it.'

He sensed his heart stopping with his nerves, feeling so alive for her, and said: 'I just love you so much.'

She said: 'Do you know what I've got for you? An ice-cold bottle of champagne in the fridge for you as your first birthday present, and two new tall glasses. I'll just run and get them.'

'Ah, wonderful wife,' he said to himself, shaking his head as he watched her dash into the kitchen. When she came back with everything and started expertly to open the bottle, he said: 'Do you know, Elenya? Do you think we could ever be separated?'

'No,' she said in a definite, serious way. 'No. That, never. But why do you ask?'

He caught her by the hands tightly and said: 'Darling, leave the champagne a second. The best present I've ever had in my life is you.'

'Oh, Kleber, don't,' she said. 'You make me want to cry with happiness.'

'Happiness is dangerous,' Kleber said. 'We're envied for it; half–real people can't understand how we found it because it's what they want themselves, don't you see?'

'Well, if people are going to be like that about such a simple thing as our happiness,' she said, 'we'll just stick tight and be buried together with it, but they'll never separate us. Never.'

'The simpler things are,' said Kleber, 'the more complicated they become.'

'Stop,' she said. 'Just let me open this bottle while it's really cold.'

'No,' said Kleber, 'we've got all night. Let me just describe how desperately I love you.'

But all he could do was hold her and gaze at her and describe what he felt with his looks; his entire being was in his eyes towards her face.

'You're making me feel faint,' she whispered, swaying.

'Hush,' he said, as he would have done to a child, holding her still and close, 'my sweet jewel, my only birthday.'

Behind them, music rang out suddenly from the radio.

'Radio Warsaw.'

'Of course.' She bent away from him temporarily to listen and said after a bit: 'It's what that bloody regime doesn't say that makes you realise what must really be going on. I'm a good Pole, Kleber, you know it, and I care about what goes on there.'

'We'll get your country back for you some day, my darling,' said Kleber, taking her by her shoulders, 'or people like us, you'll see.'

'What they've done,' said Elenya, 'well, you know what they've done. They've turned Poland into a geographical whore. There she lies, flat on her back, just as I did on Sébastopol, and Slavs don't like to be shamed.'

'I know,' said Kleber. 'Who does?'

'My parents are pathetic because they're beaten,' said Elenya. 'They slink about like whipped dogs, and if it weren't for you I'd have been another one.'

'I'm here, though.' If it weren't for Elenya it would have been impossible for Kleber to know how difficult, or even downright impossible, life was for some people in some parts of the world not too far from France.

'And thank God for it,' she said with one of the sweetest, saddest smiles he had ever seen from her. 'Now drink this bottle while it's chilled,' and she unwired it.

And so they drank to his birthday. After a while of sitting drinking and listening to a tape he badly needed to tell her what wrong he felt he had done, so all at once, as you do when you vomit, he spat it out to her about the three men he had killed.

'Something to do with Mark?'

'Yes,' said Kleber. 'I won't go into details. What you don't know can't hurt you, but I feel it's twisted me and that I was wrong to do it.'

'We're all forced into doing something wrong,' she said. She took his hand and pressed it strongly. 'Remember how I had to force my body into doing what it didn't want to?'

'It was them or Mark. Do you understand?'

'Of course I do,' she said. 'I understand anything where you're concerned, and you're not to blame yourself. You couldn't have let Mark go down.'

He drew her into his arms for her warmth again and thought, strangely, of the time when Christ had said, Take, eat, this is my body. He said: 'Don't leave me for an instant.'

Derek Raymond

She said: 'I'll never do that,' and her face melted in the face of his suffering. 'I'll never, never leave you.'

'I've crossed some great line tonight,' said Kleber, 'and I need all the help I can get.'

'I'm always here,' she said, and he felt all of her through the thin white dress she had on; and now he got the words he had in mind better as he held her: 'Christ, who in the same night that he was betrayed, took bread: and when he had given thanks, he brake it, and gave it to his disciples, saying, Take, eat, this is my body which is given for you: do this in remembrance of me. Likewise after supper he took the cup: and when he had given thanks he gave it to them, saying, Drink ye all of this, for this is my blood of the New Testament, which is shed for you... do this, as oft as ye shall drink it, in remembrance of me.'

'We'll go and make love now,' said Elenya gently, stroking his face.

And so they did, in the half-light of early day, embracing each other in that ancient magic, sobbing, sighing and kissing as we all do at such times.

Afterwards, Elenya fell asleep but Kleber found he couldn't sleep. He looked anxiously into the half-dark of their room with his right arm tight around her, imagining that he could see bores and thieves strut jauntily to their deaths. He was beginning to understand how absolute loneliness was, and for the first time began to wonder what happened to people when they ran out of ideas and time, ran out of life—these used batteries that had been men and women lay under them in their millions and he thought of how he had just contributed to them. Elenya's lips were broad in the dawn light, and

Kleber could see through the uncurtained window that
it was obviously going to rain. He also found that there
was an extremely nasty poem going through his head.
God only knows where he had heard it, or had he made
it up?:

> 'The men are all here,
> Smelling of beer;
> The girls have turned up with stinking breath,
> Including the one that played Lady Macbeth.
> So here we go, quick, quick, slow,
> Are we all ready? Isn't anyone steady?
> Are we all ready for the dance of death?
> What's that green matter?
> Who's the old squatter?
> Who brought the crow in
> On the wrist of death?
> Did you hear a patter in the court outside?
> There can't possibly be,
> I've been out to see,
> And there's nothing at all in the narrow yard,
> Nothing at all on the stones outside.
> Well, start up the singing
> And bring in those women,
> The ones in the doorway with the Scotch on
>   their breath,
> Eager and ready for the dance of death,
> Never stopping for thought or breath.
> Don't tell your dancer—it wouldn't be fair—
> To look in that mirror, for there's nothing there,
> (I tell you, dear, I can smell you from here
> As we stumble round in the dance of death.)
> Round we all reel to the songs and the chatter
> (Someone's gone down with a bang and a clatter.

> Nobody knew him so that doesn't matter.)
> But hold your fire for the dance of death
> (She's going, that girl with the web on her hat,
> 'And so I should think—God, isn't she fat?').
> We'll dance all year and drink very hard,
> And dance to death on the turn of a card.'

Nothing of what I've done is entirely my own fault, thought Kleber (he knew, of course, through being a copper that people always said that). He thought, I'm not a murderer. I killed because I had to, to protect Mark as he had asked me to. 'A true murderer doesn't suffer the way I'm doing,' he whispered; 'a person like that steps down into prison or death with a cold smile, he kills his next victim in a fit of egoism, in a psychotic, half-sexual dream—I'm not like that, am I?'

But there was the million francs in his pocket that Mark had given him. He wished now that he had never accepted them, and he decided that he would give the money back as soon as he could. He looked at his wife's sleeping body and held her tightly as she smiled and whispered in her dreams, and the mystery of her in that vague light was as deep for him as it ever had been. Her neck, her cheeks, her hair smelled so sweet to him—a natural odour that she gave off herself, unaided by any scent. He took her sleeping hand to his lips and kissed it. She stirred a little in the sheets and made a happy sound, and then at last he floated down into the darkness of his own rest. And the vast indifference of the world seemed to make his pillow almost calm as she trailed her cloudy features among his dreams.

In the afternoon Elenya woke. It was late—four o'clock. She stretched out her arms, then her legs, feeling happily used by Kleber, who slept soundly beside her.

She bent over and kissed him as she always did the minute she was awake, thinking: You're so precious, Kleber, a diamond—if you knew my tenderness. She felt it to the very ends of her. He looked so ugly and useful in his place that she found it impossible to know how far her feelings stretched for him.

And so now she got up and, without disturbing him, got dressed, making hardly any sound. She used the mirror to make up her face for what was to be the last time, thinking: I'll just slip down to the shops in the car and get him a birthday present. She was just a woman in love, but she was everything, if everything means anything. She ran out through the street door of the building, singing as she went through the little rose garden to where their car was parked—thinking for some reason of the friends she had made among the girls while she was on the street, before Kleber came, standing in doorways out of the rain, their sharp, wise tongues, the directness in their eyes. She was surprised to be thinking of them again as she went out into the cold October sunlight yet, like all people, she thought on many levels at once.

Something saddened her, passing into her like a shadow as when a cloud floats across the sun; yet she knew, thinking with a smile of Kleber, she was quite sure, that her life was very good.

Precious, fragile—but very good.

Kleber suddenly started to dream. He dreamed that he was in an old church with Elenya beside him. She was dressed as a bride and yet, as happens in dreams, also leaning across the foot of their bed and looking tenderly at him. They were back at the church; there were masses of people in it. They were nearly all old, fat, rich and in furs and diamonds—mayors, deputies and their wives, magnates, bankers and ministers, and they all disapproved of him and Elenya, looking at them coldly. They were there to be married, but the priest came up to Kleber and said: 'Aren't you ashamed of yourselves?'

'Of course not,' said Kleber, for all he could think of was Elenya's white arms and lovely hands that were stretching out to him. 'What have we got to be ashamed of? We've always been married; we've been married for ever, and now we're celebrating it.'

'You're talking too loudly,' said an old woman through pursed lips.

'Yes, so that you might understand.'

'How dare you?'

'Shut your mouth,' said Kleber. 'Shut it and pray. Don't talk.'

'It's these sorts of people who are wrecking our values!' shouted a frightful old man.

Kleber said to the priest: 'Whose side are you on, ours or theirs? Make your mind up.'

But at that moment Elenya, hushing her lips with a finger held to them, reached out to him with a bunch of white flowers she had, which moved him so much that he took her by her little waist and showed her to all the people there, saying: 'Won't any of you recognise the queen of heaven? This is your queen.'

'What an insult!' somebody said.

'No,' said Kleber. 'It's not an insult; it's the people waking and speaking. If you don't understand us, don't come anywhere near us.' He said it in such a tone that everybody in the church fell back, stunned by the gaze he had for the eyes of his woman. 'For,' he dreamed that he said, 'this is a heavenly marriage in which love is absolute; we are each other.' The priest's mouth fell open above the red and gold of his chasuble when he heard that.

'You must try to forgive us,' somebody said.

'That depends on the crimes you've committed against love,' said Kleber, leading Elenya forward. 'My lady here, she's love and so, by the contract we have between our bodies, she and I are all love in this world, for all the world.'

Then a voice groaned at him in his ear, someone who had come up behind him in the dream, yet who had nothing to do with it: 'Get up fast. Get dressed. Do it now and come down.'

He was already out of bed and had his trousers on. He rushed out of the door and at that instant the bomb in the car went off, and it was the fact that he was already in the hall that saved his life. He sailed down on its red blast, whirled round by it, falling, to find himself leaning against the wall by the street door shoe deep in dead leaves and broken glass. He shook his head, pulled himself together and was amazed to find that nothing had happened to him except that he no longer had any clothes on. So, dazed, he went out into the rose garden naked, not knowing what he was doing except that he had to find Elenya, though he knew all too well what had happened to her. His eyes were shut at first as he went out into the garden—it was the shock—but when he managed to open them he saw that his wife's flesh was hanging and dripping in the rose thorns, and he perceived that it wouldn't be possible for him to be kind to anybody again now. He knelt, naked, and reached out around him for pieces of her smoking flesh. 'You'll be sneered at in heaven itself if you don't get all of her back now, right away,' he kept saying to himself. But there was no means by which he could do it; he ran round and round the garden trying to recognise the lumps of her, and he didn't know that he was crying and screaming, with her blood running through his hands—for Elenya, not three minutes before, had turned the key in the starter of the car which had been wired to a bomb intended for Kleber, and now the police and ambulance people were already coming up. That was just as well, because there was nothing left of the car at all but a twisted chassis and three wheels. He sought to pick all of her up but she was much too spread about, hanging in the thorns—her left hand—and on the grass like that, so that he couldn't hope to get her back, yet at the same moment she was still back with him, together, in the world she had just quit. She was saying to him: 'You know, I'm just a little drag-horse, Kleber, a flounder, a little mule—I'll do your washing, cook your supper, bear your children if I can still have any, because you brought my honour back to me and dressed me in white again for the world. My dignity's renewed through you, and I can no longer be bought and sold on a street corner.' Thinking of her, and looking for all of her in the garden, tears started out of Kleber; he had never known what agony such crying could be.

And at the third hour Christ screamed and said: Oh, Father, take this cup from me. But they could not, and Kleber knew it, and so now he screamed too, and went on doing so until a young doctor took him by the arm. They put a sedative into it to calm Kleber and then, having discussed him for a time, carried him up and put him in the ruins of the bed in which he had made love with Elenya only such a short time before—so short that the sheets were still warm from their bodies.

Meantime, in the street, in the little garden, the work

of picking up the bits of her went on, as all things somehow must.

Some time in the night Elenya came to Kleber in his drugged sleep and said to him: 'I'm not dead, darling; we're not apart. You know that.'

He got up hours later; he had no idea at first what time it could be. Still only half in his mind he went in a mechanical way to go through to the kitchen, forgetting that he had lost her and hoping to find her making the coffee as she usually did. But in so doing he pierced his feet on the masses of glass where the whole front of their flat had fallen inwards, and for the first time, really, noticed the terrible state of the place. For no reason whatever he found himself thinking of old people: a retired man coughing into a fire to conceal the evidence of his coming death, the expiring gasp of a fart from an old woman in a bar. He was still partly, though moving about around the wreckage of his life, in his drugged sleep and proclaimed, but silently: 'A thousand shall fall beside thee, and ten thousand at thy right hand, but they shall not come nigh thee.'

'You'll come back, darling,' he said up to her where she was in the ceiling. Of course, this was completely wrecked and the windows had all come into the place, which was howling and freezing with draughts. It was the first time he had ever done it, but Kleber wrung his hands: 'We'll meet again,' he said.

'Of course we will,' she said to him suddenly. 'I was a good girl, and no bomb can destroy me or ever could.'

Traces of the fingerprint dust that the police always left everywhere, whatever they were doing on a death, and also some of the postcards that he and Elenya sent each other on the few occasions they were apart, lay scattered about on the floor and Kleber turned away from it all. He decided that he would get out of the place at once and never go back, but as he turned to leave the room he noticed, on the floor, a little crushed cartwheel-shaped hat that she had bought down on the beach at Narbonne during their holidays last summer, and he somehow couldn't stop himself picking it up and holding it at an angle so that he could suppose that her head was still in it (though the forensic people hadn't been able to find her head). The hat had a red flower in its band, and Kleber picked it up and put it carefully into the bag he was taking with him. He didn't take much—just what he needed for the present, a few shirts and a razor, enough to cut the past off. He went through what was left of the door and out. Her flesh had been cleared away from the garden now and everyone had gone. It was a clean sort of day but raining hard, and he glanced at his watch, which told him that it was the day after his birthday. He waited for a 38 bus, nodding at the bright advertisements in the shelter. The bus arrived and he got on it, staring at the vast sadness of life as it sped away backwards from him in the window.

Later the same day he rang his mother-in-law. He didn't expect her to understand much of what he said, or why he said it, and she didn't. But he told her: 'There's been this accident to Elenya, and she's dead.'

'I know,' said the old woman. 'It's in the papers.' She spoke in her broken Polish-French.

'It was all my fault,' said Kleber, 'and I'm afraid I will never be the same again, Mrs Kucharski.'

'What do you mean?' she said. 'Was she really all that

important to you?'

'Yes,' said Kleber. 'She was.'

'She wasn't a very clever girl.'

'If you analyse cleverness hard enough,' said Kleber savagely, 'you'll generally find stupidity and selfishness under it.'

'I don't understand what you're saying.'

'I know you don't,' said Kleber.

'Don't involve her father,' she implored. 'He's got a weak heart.'

'We all have,' said Kleber, 'but the problem is, some of us have got weak heads to go with them,' and he rang off. Turning away from the telephone box and out into the street again, Kleber watched the city for a moment under its dark daylight, watched men and women around him planning to murder and make love.

Next he went into a café and rang the morgue where there was a man he knew, who told him exactly what they had been able to find of her. Kleber listened patiently to the recital and at the end said politely: 'Thank you very much.'

They had found some of her hair, which had been flowing on the pillow next to him only shortly before, and her beautiful left hand intact, but the rest of her was much less obvious and better not gone into. Kleber's problem was that he didn't know what on earth he was going to do without her—in fact, right at this moment he didn't know how he was going to do anything at all, apart, of course, from getting hold of the man who had killed her, or had her killed. She had gone to her death in a white flash through his own fault. He should never have allowed himself to sleep like that after what he had done with Mark. The fact that he had been a copper, the fact that the bomb had been meant for him, all that made

Derek Raymond

it still worse, if there could be anything worse. The police had scooped her up with spades and put what they had been able to find into those special bags of theirs.

It was quite a little body that he had made love to only yesterday, he recollected now. With hindsight, he saw her much more clearly now. Her arms had really been quite little arms, but they were tender enough, if people were only prepared to understand what the loss of her meant, to put the whole world in tears. They had found one of her cheeks in the rose bushes, his friend at the morgue had told him, but it would be hard to stroke it now.

'Dead by my negligence,' he muttered, 'when it was my trade to be alert.' And later: 'She's gone. Gone. And somehow or other you've got to try to learn to understand exactly what that means, Kleber.'

10

Kleber was in a bar on Sébastopol, looking, watching, waiting for his wife's killer. Absently he listened to the jukebox which was moaning:

> 'What's the use of waiting, baby,
> When we know it ain't no use?'

Suddenly Elenya was beside him in his mind—it was so sudden that Kleber upset his kir. She murmured to him:

> 'Now we can tread the stateliest dance of all,
> And turn each other slowly in our hands
> As we did in the old days, darling.'

She left him. Kleber thought again of Sickert's work on whores. Why was it only now that he realised that those dark marks on their faces under their cheap nineteenth-century hats were caused by smallpox and syphilis as well as bruises created by dissatisfied customers?

How cruel it is in life that disaster should set you apart from everybody.

Not quite, though. Several little villains surrounded Kleber, one of them with a beer in his hand. He upset this over Kleber. It went over his shirt and the man said: 'That's a free one, you busted cunt, and it's a pleasure for me to buy it for you.'

'Are you always kind to people like that when they're down?' said Kleber. 'I think we ought to work out something a bit special for you. What do you think?'

The man hesitated, realising too late that he didn't know Kleber as well as he thought he did. Kleber said: 'It's all right. It's just an old shirt I've got on. It's too old for me to care how it's treated.' He added: 'But you mightn't be.'

One of the other men said: 'I think I should leave him alone if I were you, Willy.'

'Why? He's just a busted size nine in hats.'

'Maybe, but his wife was blown to bits yesterday.'

'How I enjoy listening to little thieves and grasses chattering on,' said Kleber.

'My name's Willy,' said the man, stubbing his cigarette out quietly on Kleber's knee.

'Well,' said Kleber calmly, 'I suppose you've got to be called something.' He brushed the red-hot cinders off himself.

'You mean that little Polish bat you had?' asked Willy.

'I should be very, very careful what you're saying,' said Kleber, 'if I were you.'

'Why?' said Willy. He felt confident because he had his friends with him, and nudged one of them in the ribs, laughing. 'I like it when busted coppers' birds take a short fever.'

'I don't insist on it,' said Kleber, 'but this is a big bar, and I should just leave me alone in it if I were you.'

But the idiot wouldn't. He said to Kleber: 'You look as if you could do with a new ankle, darling.' And kicked him on one of them with his solid boot, whereon Kleber sighed, got slowly to his feet and said: 'I did warn you.' He hit the man across the throat with the edge of his hand so hard that as he fell the people around him thought he was going to die; his face and neck, as he collapsed, turned red, then purple and black.

'Clear that away,' said Kleber to the others. 'He's not going to be any use to anyone any more.'

The barman ran along to Kleber and said: 'That's enough of that.'

'It certainly is for some people,' said Kleber. 'Have a look at the man on the floor. And if you want to make yourself useful for once, I should ring the hospital.'

'Don't look for any more trouble.'

'I don't need to,' said Kleber. 'I've just had a very serious death in the family and I want to be alone with my thoughts, if that's all right.'

Nobody contradicted him, which was extremely sensible of them; one of the men who had been with Willy made a phone call from the bar and presently a battered 305 with a front wing missing drove up and they picked Willy up, carried him away and put him in it. Some snot and filth that Willy had left lay behind him on the floor.

Kleber never had any more trouble in that bar after that. He left, after telling the barman who he was looking for and why. But as he went out he was remembering a time when he had seen Elenya on their bed on a hot night, her knees drawn up in sleep and her back to him. She looked so defenceless that he had felt afraid.

And he was right to have been afraid.

He could only half-hear Elenya's music now; it was becoming erased. He looked up to the sky from the street. It was getting dark and Paris seemed to him nothing but a cluster of dirty brilliants hung around a dark and absent wrist. He recited to himself:

'I'll read a paper soon and see my eyes
In that mad, careful print accused.
Which year? What men? Whose cause?
Aren't all times fused in pain?
For now we can tread the prettiest dance of all
And state our pace towards the edge of death,
Dancing to darkness...'

He knew that he was only half himself now. He walked on, remembering so strongly what he had whispered to her in the night in the first days they knew each other in their arms: 'What brilliance you are! But how can I capture you in my hands without bruising your wings or else cutting my hands on them?' But he remembered that she was asleep and moaned in it at the time, tossing away from him in the bed. Kleber remembered how staggering an experience love had been when it came to a man like himself, solitary by nature, a man who liked to have every single thing in his life under his own control, and how he had become completely unspun, wrung by Elenya, wrung out like a rag by his feelings for her when they met, so that he had said to her when they were sitting on a café terrace soon after: 'You know, all I want to do is to hold you in my arms twenty-four hours out of twenty-four; you distract me as much by your presence as your absence. When you're with me I can't seem to think any more about what I'm saying; you drink me up with your eyes—and when you're not there I wish I were being drunk up into your eyes.'

He recalled that conversation with her so clearly: their love with its arms open coming to each other for them. 'How many years, centuries,' he wondered now, 'before I see you and hold you again?'

Suddenly she was there beside him, holding his hand

firmly in hers. 'Only a little time, darling, but find me quickly because I'm lost here without you.'

It seemed to Kleber that their hands were as solidly together as they had ever been.

'But when?' he said. 'How soon?'

'Ah, no,' she said, 'it won't be long but don't ask—for one question only provokes another; there can never be any answers.'

'Then I've never understood anything,' said Kleber.

'Be calm,' she said. 'You will soon be changed from head to foot.'

'At least always be near me when I am going through this,' he said, and she whispered back: 'Where else could I ever be?'

She left him. What is tragedy? thought Kleber, walking through it in the streets. For him, it was the loss of that warm thigh that he had placed his hand on when he was home and had finished for the day—their meals, walking arm in arm in the street, nudging each other in the cinema, such silly, obvious things, or else her lips and all her soul and flesh against him when they made love, just the things that people do to assure the movement of our world.

'Always be near me,' said Kleber, 'and then perhaps your absence won't seem so bad.' But she didn't answer, and Kleber walked on with his head bent towards the everlasting rain. He walked in a state of vast sadness that she was no longer to be found anywhere in the world, shedding the loss of her through mad tears; for she had been him, as no other human being ever could be, or would again—and so the conditions of our existence, he concluded for the time being, break us all down in the end.

And so now he accepted, finally, that she had definitely

gone: it was the agony of being dragged apart from one's own flesh. It was as if, he pictured it, she had left on a great train that was as long as misery itself, a train which pulled out into darkness—night itself being as long, dark and profound as misery. He dreamed as he walked that he saw her leave, her little head leaning out of the carriage window, smiling at him in its beauty, youth and disarray, for those few seconds before she left for the unknown.

A man in clothes that were too bright came up behind Kleber and pulled him by the arm. It was a silly thing to have done, seeing the mood that Kleber was in just then. When Kleber spoke to him his tone was low, but it sounded like someone loading a pistol—a series of precise, metallic and fatal noises.

'Don't bore me,' said Kleber, 'and never take a man by the arm from behind otherwise look what happens to you.' For Kleber had had enough of being an ex-copper and was sick of little thieves sniggering at him or coming up on him from behind. So he took the man into his embrace, drove the heel of his boot into his instep and said: 'Now you can't get away from me, can you, because you can't fucking walk. Pity for you you ever came near me in the first place.' While the man yelled with pain, Kleber frisked him with his free hand, found the knife he had on him and threw it down a drain. 'Now what are you going to do?' said Kleber conversationally. 'I'll answer the question for you: you're going to stand still and get hurt some more, and then perhaps the word'll get around that I want to be left alone.' He took the man by his hair and banged his face into the street wall very hard. The man screamed, struggling with all his might to get away from Kleber, but he might as well have struggled to escape from a boa-constrictor.

'You're looking a bit less cheeky now,' said Kleber. He stared into the man's eyes, which were full of the blood dribbling down his hair. 'Now, when you're able to hobble to a shop and buy a stick to walk with, go back and tell your friends never, ever to try anything like that on me again—it might be more serious next time, might even be a funeral job. Talking of that, there's just been a very, very serious death in my family, and may the living Christ help you or anyone else who knows a single thing about it. And also warn the man whose face I know, who likes raping women and blowing them to bits, that I'm after him extremely hard. Now fuck off.' And Kleber threw him out into the middle of the street, so that was the end of that.

11

Kleber waited near his old headquarters and said to the man he wanted as he hurried out of the door: 'Hello.' Kleber was very close to him.

'I'm not supposed to talk to you.'

Kleber's hand closed over his ex-colleague's wrist.

'I'm just going off-duty,' said this detective. 'I've got to be going.'

'And I know where to,' said Kleber. 'It's payday, isn't it? It's come around again, hasn't it? The way it does every month—now don't be a cunt and listen to me.'

'I haven't time. I've got to be on my way.'

'I know you've got time,' said Kleber, 'because I'm making sure you're not going to have any. Now which are you going to do? Give me the information I want or get busted?'

'I don't know what you mean.'

'You don't need to,' said Kleber, 'because I know exactly what I mean. Three men died last night who worked for the man you're about to draw your wages from to help pay for that new Mercedes you've got, and if you're not fucking careful you might well be the fourth.' He added: 'I've had my eye on you for a year, you bent bastard. Where are you meeting him? In some bar?'

'I'm not meeting anyone except my bird,' the detective shouted. 'Now let go of me.'

'Just tell me where he is,' said Kleber in a tone so sinister that the other man would have looked for cover if Kleber hadn't been holding him by the arm. 'You ought to know, since he's making you so rich.'

'I don't know, I tell you!'

'You're lying,' said Kleber, 'but then you are a fucking liar.'

'You couldn't get me busted anyway,' said the other man. 'You're busted yourself.'

Kleber slapped him carelessly in the balls. The man screamed, but it was dark and raining, and there was so much noise in the street that no one could have heard him even if they had cared, and there they were, the two of them, apparently talking amicably outside the police station.

'You know what happened to my wife, don't you?' said Kleber.

'I heard, yes.'

'Of course you fucking well heard,' said Kleber. 'You could hardly have helped it in your job, could you? Now if you want to live to draw your pension you'd better tell me where the man is who's paying you—the man where you look the other way when his heroin comes in.'

'Christ, you've hurt me,' said the detective, trying to straighten up in Kleber's grip and tenderly massaging his balls with his other hand.

'I've hurt you because you needed hurting,' said Kleber. 'Now talk.'

'It'd be a death sentence.'

'Then that means that you've got two of them hanging over you, you poor sod, his and mine. I'll give you until this time tomorrow to tell me what I want to know, otherwise I'll go to the press with what I know about you, and your career will look like something that's been forgotten in the frying pan.'

'All right,' said the detective as Kleber released him. 'Perhaps you'd like it if we both went and met him.' He caressed his wrist.

'No,' said Kleber. 'It's bad policy to kill a man in a bar—you just remember to tell him that it'll happen to him somewhere else. Yes, you just remember to tell him that, darling,' Kleber said as he walked away, and he thought as he looked back and watched the detective, still stooping, going off in the other direction: you poor slave.

Kleber remembered, as he walked along, that he had often thought about Elenya in her lifetime: what would happen to me, darling, if you died? Now he knew. It meant the crushing of all hope; now he really didn't care what he said or did to anyone any more. He was destroyed in his loss—the loss of Elenya appeared to him to be the loss of all mankind. I won't get over this, Kleber thought; if I do, it's going to be a very narrow affair; all I can do is look for the strength to act—for he knew that he had to do that to get back to Elenya. The problem now was to find the means and courage to do it; because of everything that had happened he suddenly found himself up against all the evil, everything that was wrong with the world concentrated in his own, isolated heart.

'By my negligence!' he groaned in the street. 'And it was my trade not to be. Is there no tenderness, no love in the world? Doesn't anyone care for the value of the wife I've just lost? Don't they care about their own wives? How much do they care, these people passing me in the street?'

He walked on up the great boulevard through the rain until he came to a bar whose lights glowed out against the wet. He went in—the place was full of winter tourists sitting at tables not talking to each other. Kleber said to himself: 'These people don't understand anything at all; they might as well not be alive. They put no value on anything or anyone whatever, you can see it, these tedious fools, not even on each other.'

So he turned towards them and gave them all the fascist salute. The barman rushed over to him and shouted: 'What did you do that for?'

'Just to see what would happen,' said Kleber, 'and look, nothing has, except that the people who were pink have now turned white, and the pale ones have turned the other colour.'

'I know you,' said the barman. 'You're that busted copper. OK, but what's the matter with you? Are you drunk, ill or what? Look, you're emptying my place!'

For people were herding each other out of the door in embarrassment.

'They were on a tour of Paris,' said the barman furiously.

'Well, now they've discovered Paris, haven't they?' said Kleber. 'I'm the sort of thing that intelligent people come here to see.' He shouted after the last departing figures: 'My wife's just been blown to bits and what the fucking hell do any of you care about it? Now get back in your fucking bus.' He said to the barman: 'Bang go your profits, but you can't have truth and money at the same time.'

'I don't want any fucking truth!' the barman screamed.

'I can see that,' said Kleber, 'but the trouble is, you can't always choose. If you see the man who's responsible for my wife's death, you'd better tell me if you know what's good for you. I'll be back.'

He went out, slamming the door so hard that a pane of glass broke.

12

The next day Kleber found himself in a *pension* off the Boulevard de Sébastopol called L'Hôtel du Bourg. It wasn't anything special and there were no formalities. Living in it were a number of Arabs, old writers, queens and people whose trade you couldn't put any name to. At times bursts of music came out of some room on the first floor, but at night it was mostly silence coupled with the occasional quarrel and the insistent noise of rain pattering on the roof, which was just above Kleber's room on the fourth floor. Kleber lay there sometimes for an hour or two when he was exhausted or wanted to think; he never slept now. He had his suitcase with his few things in it at the end of the bed and Elenya's straw hat on the shabby old armchair, where he could see it from the bed. He never got into bed; he didn't feel things like heat or cold now. He just lay on it, approaching other questions slowly, looking at the cracks in the faded plaster of the ceiling. He seemed to himself to be more of a notion of a man than a real one as he lay there; he was a difference between two states—neither one nor the other. The situation he was in, which of course he had created, would be resolved where he ended, but he already felt like an exercise on paper for eager students to pore over and discuss. He felt that if he were to cut himself now he wouldn't even bleed. He felt like a man who was going to be hanged in the morning and had resigned himself to it. He felt quite indifferent about his existence in a way; it was, he supposed, the only attitude by means of which he could accept that his existence now no longer meant anything to him. While he rested on the bed with his arms supporting his neck, he would softly whistle the notes of the signature tune of Radio Warsaw, which Elenya had so loved, in E-major; Kleber had once been an excellent whistler. But now he was indifferent to the sound his lips made because there was no one to listen to it; he just noted idly, almost, that he had got it right. He was hard put to arm himself against his loneliness, and indeed never managed it.

At one moment Elenya appeared to him in his mind as he lay like that and murmured: 'All our love will come back to us again, you'll see. But fight for us both now, Kleber: I can't describe to you how important it is, for our joint power is in your hands now.'

'Then pray for us, darling,' Kleber said aloud, and she whispered back: 'My sweetheart, I do nothing else.'

Later she said to him: 'I'm right beside you, Kleber. I know you can manage. Feel me. Can't you feel my hand in yours? My arm? My cheek against you?'

Kleber could. He could even smell her faint, familiar odour. She felt and looked like no other woman he had ever known and he replied: 'Of course. Yes, I can feel and hear you.'

'Then don't give up now, Kleber,' Elenya said, 'whatever you do, not even if you feel you're in the final corner of your life.'

'I won't,' Kleber said, 'believe me. Just swear you'll always be there and we'll be all right.' He reached his arms out to the empty air, yet still felt her in them. He wondered what it would have been like to have got to, say, the age of eighty, with all the music you had ever loved played through dusty tapes on half-broken machines while you lay or stayed still with no one to look after you, no one to look after what was left of you, and no one to care about what you had learned. He thought that must be the worst thing that our strange condition had to offer, and thought that he would rather be nothing, like Elenya was, than have to undergo that. Old people in cafés fumbling through the photographs of their young or dead, spilling them on to wine-stained tables out of old wallets to poke them under the noses of uninterested, uninvolved people, was that what existence came down to? Was there nothing more to the appalling risk of living than that? No reward at all? Elenya had been blown to pieces, and yet the meaningless jangle of life went on; people playing tennis in other places, planting, mowing, banking, smoking and drinking, gossiping. Yet the value of one life, he felt sure, must be the value of any life.

Presently he got up and went down into the street. Elenya said to him: 'Be brave, sweetheart—we'll meet again.'

'I want it now,' he said to her. 'Now.'

'We can't.'

She left him and he walked off into the rain. He reflected on everything he had ever seen in the course of his work that he remembered—objects such as cheap milk jugs thrown into corners in the rooms of murdered people, every tragic sight that he had ever been forced to witness: shit on carpets, blind, dead eyes that would gaze on past the living until they rotted, old eyes that nobody wanted, nobody needed, eyes that the living could make no use of, eyes that had never really been looked into, eyes that now studied their own infinity. He heard all life in his tears, listened to it in his grief and, because even pain must have an end, Kleber felt that it was now really better to run on it, have it over. He wished in the hopeless way that the bereaved have that her death had happened to him, who was built, fitted for it, even ready for it through the work he had chosen, and been chosen for something stronger in himself than he could control, and not to Elenya. She had already had enough with her loaded past, but he was obsessed with the conviction that he had not protected her enough—they had made love on his birthday and he had afterwards slept on the battlements while the castle had been forced. So she had died in a horrible way, like an unlucky woman falling off a roof.

In those few moments where his pain eased as he lay unsleeping on the bed, he imagined her as though she was still recoverable: she looked so elegant to him as she entered through a door at the edge of his desperate sleep, reaching out to him in a red dress she had once bought to surprise him with at dinner; it was a dress that showed off her excellent legs and small breasts, and there was nothing so completely cruel in what was left for him than the sweetness she bore in her looks towards him now that she was dead. In his brief dream of her she still lived: indeed, was better, more brilliant than when she had been alive, and he watched her smiling, leaning over his bed to say: 'I have come to tell you, dearest, that we shall soon be together for ever.'

When that happened he sat up with a shock, hitting his head against the wall. But he knew it wasn't time for him to go yet.

In the street she murmured to him, I beg only one thing of you from where I am now: protect me, your dead, for if you don't then my hands can't reach out to you.

Closing his eyes he saw her in her new white beauty; he was sure he saw her as he walked up Sébastopol under the persistent rain, imagining her lost face. She said: 'Always remember that your strength is as great as ours; give it to me now when it's needed.'

He answered: 'I have.'

'Only do that,' she said, 'and my love shall print its name on your lips.'

'I'm going out over to the other side,' said Kleber, and passers-by turned to look curiously at him as he went by, at his working mouth.

13

Kleber found that he was in a bar on Sébastopol. 'Somebody's body isn't just something you take,' he said to the man on the stool next to him; 'it has to be given to you.'

'Who's this lunatic?' said the man.

'Just a busted copper,' said the barman. 'I wouldn't pay any attention to him if I were you.'

'It's hard not to.'

'I was thinking of throwing him out,' said the barman. 'The only trouble is, it's not that simple to do.'

Apart from the three of them, the bar was almost empty because it was late. Kleber said: 'What do you think the secret of love really is?'

'It's the wrong time of night to start talking of things like that,' the barman said. 'I'm closing.'

'I know all about your licence,' Kleber said, 'and there's no rush on for that in your case. Have you ever seen horses having a fuck?'

They hadn't. 'When I was a child,' said Kleber, 'down at my grandparents'. The female's on heat, and you can tell by her eyes that she isn't sure if she wants that particular stallion or not, but she's got no choice because she's fettered down and the stallion, who will screw anything and fancies himself rotten, has her anyway, while the owners stand by hoping that the foal's going to make them money. Transfer all that to people and we call it a society.'

The few people who were still in the bar got up at that

and left without looking at anybody, not even each other.

'That's it,' said the barman, 'I'm definitely shutting now.'

'Sit down,' said Kleber coldly, 'before you get a headache from running about. Did you know,' he said to the man next to him, 'how much sperm goes into a mare? I'll bet you don't.'

'No,' said the man. 'I don't. And I don't care.'

'I thought not,' said Kleber. 'Anyway, the answer is, more than a litre. It's a funny sort of colour, too, yellowish, but not like piss—thicker, you know.'

'We're not that particular about conversation in here,' said the barman, 'and I've heard most things, but are you leaving right now or am I going to have to put you out?'

'I'm afraid so,' said Kleber. 'I'm afraid for your sake, because you're going to wind up wishing you hadn't tried. Now, as I was saying, animals are put to each other for money just like people are; the only difference is that we wear clothes.'

'Why don't I laugh at this man if he's so funny?' the man beside Kleber said.

'I've no idea,' said Kleber. 'Probably because you're a bore.'

At the same time as he was speaking Kleber was looking back at all the experiences in his past that he had been only half able to understand until he met Elenya, wondering: has it all been worth it? What? Just for this? A dead wife, a ruined career, one lout and one bore at a counter? What was her life worth? What was his life worth?

The question tormented him, so he paid up and left, whistling the notes of Radio Warsaw. But in the street he thought: each life, each death is a catastrophe. The more you love a life, love someone, the more special, precious that person becomes for you and the more fragile that life is. The more you want to protect someone, the more you need to protect them, and the more you realise that they stand in need of protection. The loss of her was so great that now, inside himself, Kleber could only stare and weep. Inside Kleber now he was just a funeral that carried on twenty-four hours a day. After all, he thought, if you didn't mourn what you had loved, what would you do? Buy a new car? A handful of flowers, perhaps—nothing too expensive. The loss of Elenya was all the more strange to Kleber, too, because he had never been a man who had found it easy to love. By nature he had no time for fools or weakness, so that when he did go overboard for someone he went the complete distance. Where I live best, he thought, is at the centre of total change, no matter how agonising, and here I am again, right in it. It brings *me* out, the *what* I am of myself, my values.

'I'm wide awake, darling,' Elenya said in the dark street. 'Can you feel me?'

He could. He said: 'Give me courage, because I shall need all that I can get to repair the error.'

She whispered: 'But it is repaired. There wasn't any error, and we're both very much less further off from each other than you think.'

But he could only answer: 'Farewell, my goddess, my treasure, my own and only sweet existence. Oh, my darling, how I cry over my vast loss of you. Have I gone mad?'

But she said: 'Ah, no, prince—for now I, being invisible to you for a time, am real but different and in a different sense.'

*

Now she was knocking at the door of his hotel room where he had gone to try to rest. There was the most dreadful sound in the knocking.

'Let me in, Kleber,' she whispered. 'It's me. Please let me in. Please.'

'But the door's open!' he screamed.

'I can't get in, darling!'

'But you must!'

In the rooms around him people began to stir, wake up and complain.

Oh, uneasy ghost, poor unquiet and troubled spirit, lie in peace at last with all our love. For the mad and the dead lead their secret lives just as we do, suffer, have longings and love just as we do. They can't explain it, but then perhaps explanations don't really matter so much after all—not when you compare the feeling to the words.

'Come back!' Kleber shouted. 'Come back, darling.'

'I'm here.'

But he turned his face to the wall, saying: 'I'm sick with my tears, my red tears.'

The four friends in the arms of the prince had been eating, drinking and talking during his absence. Why was it that they were asleep when the castle was stormed and taken?

How did Kleber think of such a thing?

He must have been dreaming.

He realised that Elenya had always been too beautiful to live. Meaninglessly born into a violent, horrible and squalid world, no one but he had been even faintly capable of understanding her, and anyway it was too late now; she was dead.

He wondered how he could go on, what he would do now. Only he didn't care what he did—he had already changed his identity.

When he was himself again he found that his face was covered with blood. He looked for the reason why that was so and found it on the wall beside the bed; he had beaten his head against it, there were great smears on it. He placed his fingers absently on his own blood, wondering what it had to do with he value of a human life.

Yes, the friends of the prince, through nothing more serious than an hour's negligence, had let the castle be taken, and the others had captured his queen and killed her.

It was the year 1600 all over again: nothing had changed.

14

Kleber found himself in an all-night bar on Sébastopol leaning on the counter.

'I'm not serving you,' said the barman.

'Why not?'

'Because you're bad news.'

'For some people I am,' Kleber nodded. 'You know who I'm looking for?'

'No, I don't,' said the barman. 'I'm not paid to know things. Anyway, even if I did know, what do you want him for?'

'I want to pay him what I owe him. I always pay my debts.'

The owner of the bar came over and said: 'Serve Kleber. Do it now.'

Kleber said: 'A kir.'

When he was served, Kleber said to the owner: 'I expect you've heard that I'm looking for the man who was so kind to my wife yesterday?'

'No, all I heard was that you'd been suspended. What do you mean, he was kind to your wife?'

'Three men were shot down in the street last night.'

'Oh, them,' said the owner. 'Cheers. Well, they're probably no great loss.'

'No,' said Kleber, 'probably not. But my wife's a great loss.'

'What happened to her?'

'You never read the papers,' said Kleber, 'that's your trouble. Well, she was blown to bits by a car bomb in

113

my car.'

'I'm very sorry to hear that,' said the owner.

'I was sorry to hear it too,' said Kleber. 'Made an extremely loud bang.'

'She was a nice girl. I remember her. Very pretty.'

'Yes,' said Kleber, 'wasn't she?'

'She was Polish,' said the barman. 'Is that the one? Used to work the—'

'Don't stick your nose in where it isn't wanted,' said the owner. 'Fuck off, shithead, or you'll be looking for another job.' He said to Kleber: 'Look, try not to be so difficult.'

'I can't seem to help it somehow,' said Kleber. 'I'm going through difficult times.'

'Aren't we all?'

'To cause the death of others is a truly terrible thing,' said Kleber. 'In fact, I sometimes wonder why I'm ever alive, myself. My wife sometimes used to wonder the same thing.'

'Look,' said the owner, staring into his drink, 'I think I might be able to arrange something like a meeting. Only you've got to be reasonable.'

'I'm afraid I don't feel very reasonable.'

'You'll have to make an effort if I fix this up.'

'Why are you even trying?'

'Because there does seem to have been a mistake.'

'You're right,' said Kleber. 'It was a fatal mistake.'

'All the same, what's done is done.'

'Maybe,' said Kleber, 'but it's not by any means over, if you see what I'm driving at.'

'I can arrange a talk,' the owner said. 'I think you ought to just speak to the man. You know, have a quick word.'

'What for?'

'Well, you know, fix things up amicably.'

'What's the point of talking to the dead?' said Kleber.

'I don't understand.'

'Look,' said Kleber. 'I'm after him. He's as good as dead.'

The owner said: 'What's this money people say you owe him?'

'Well,' said Kleber, 'they put pennies over dead men's eyes, don't they?'

He finished his drink and left.

He went out into the street to think and walk about, for it was written for him, in his misery, in a special book, that though you could kick love to death it would always come back searching for you; it would always be remembered and replaced—somewhere—especially if its loss were none of your fault. So Kleber went out into the dark and the rain to hear love somehow reheard and renewed, however little time he had left to him to understand its music, and in the hope that no agony could ever conquer love. For it seemed to him that human life was made up of such small, tattered convictions, which sounded banal when stated, yet which turned out to be absolutely vital and of supreme importance, especially when the great crisis came on—death—or when it was about to come on: you suddenly thought of an old telephone number, and then all the values were suddenly unburied again—there was the memory as fresh as if it were only yesterday, of a book that a friend had lent you which had excited your mind, or else it was a long kiss under a lamp, or your furious nerves as you waited for a girl with long legs, sweet eyes and elegant hands to arrive, or it could be some crucial news you were waiting for. A friend of Kleber's had once killed himself over a girl who had betrayed him, but not before he had pressed the only treasure he had—a penknife with an ivory handle—into Kleber's hand. Kleber had been too young to understand the importance of the gesture and had long ago lost the knife, having left it by accident on a restaurant table among the fruit peelings.

He walked up Sébastopol thinking: All that I loved is dead, a condition that gives you exaggerated moods. He knew that he would have to have all the faith that he could summon up if Elenya were ever to be returned to him—but then everything was an act of faith, if everything was anything.

Even so, he found himself saying into the darkness: 'I may not make it. I mightn't pull through this time.'

But Elenya whispered to him: 'I'll help you with my arms, darling. I'll pull you through.'

But you were dead before you had a chance to understand. Why?

There were times, when he was thinking about Elenya, that he believed he had his arm around the waist of the whole world. Anyway, you couldn't escape pain, he knew that—you could only face it. It was somehow only in that way that you could be changed from head to foot, and that was what he wanted. Yes, what Kleber wanted was to be back again in his really quite small but real world—to get his loved ones back, to recover all of them, and indeed anyone, anywhere, with whom he would have enjoyed having a drink, no matter how far, like himself, they had strayed off this strange path. What transcending beauty.

'The best things,' said Kleber, 'are written in a script that you can only half-read.' All the roughness of his life was suddenly swept away as he sat thinking about Elenya by a vast wave of love for her. He found himself thinking about lives he had seen that had been snuffed out. Who knows? Their owners might have wanted to live.

He muttered this half-aloud and the man sitting next to him at the bar said: 'What's the matter with you?'

'What do you mean?' said Kleber.

'Well, you seemed to be crying,' the man said, 'if you don't mind my saying so.'

'Was I?' said Kleber. 'Well, I daresay I was right to do it.'

'Got a problem, have you?'

'I have rather.'

'Want to talk about it?'

'I don't mind, I suppose,' said Kleber. 'Does one good to talk sometimes, doesn't it?'

'Well, then?'

Kleber said: 'My wife's just been blown to bits by a bomb, that's what the matter is, and I was rather trying to think how I might get back to her, if you know what I mean. The trouble was, I loved her, which may have been stupid of me.' He remembered how he had lain in bed with her one summer in a small room they had rented in the south, made love, laughed, and watched the sunlight moving slowly across the floor—such other times, yet they had only had a chance to spend four years together. But those four years were worth all eternity.

The man was pretty shattered and managed to say: 'Christ, when did that happen?'

'Only yesterday,' said Kleber, 'but it seems much longer ago than that. And yet not—at other times it seems to me only five minutes, or no minutes. When she went off with a bang like that I somehow got out into the garden, found myself there naked, and there were all the bits of

117

her dripping in the bushes, you know, and it was all my fault because I was asleep when I shouldn't have been, and didn't hear her go out to get the car. You see, yesterday it was my birthday and we'd been making love, and I was so tired after it that I fell asleep when I shouldn't have done, and now I can't repair the mistake, and that's why I'm pretty disturbed, you see. But what would you have done in my place? What could anybody have done?'

'I can't think,' the man said. 'God, it's unbelievable.'

'Unfortunately,' said Kleber, 'it's not.'

'I don't think I could take it,' said the man. 'Here, have a drink at least.'

'Thanks,' said Kleber. He added: 'Oh, I can take it. Look, you can see me sitting here and taking it. I'm taking it because I've got to take it. You've got to take it because it's happened. I've got one piece of luck still— she speaks to me all the time. What I did in the garden was, before the police had a chance to arrive, I filled my hands and arms with her flesh and blood and added my tears to them.'

'Jesus Christ.'

'Yes, that's the problem,' Kleber said. 'You make one mistake, just one, and it's your last. It can't be repaired.'

'It would drive me mad.'

'Unluckily for me,' said Kleber, 'I can't go mad. I only hear her voice, of course—I can't really see her or feel her, I only think I can. You know, it's like losing a leg and thinking you've still got it.'

'What do you do for a living?'

'I draw my pay,' said Kleber, 'anyway for a while.'

'What else?'

'Oh, I'm busy moving, as usual,' said Kleber, 'getting all my gear together, you know. Packing up to leave, getting rid of all the rubbish.'

'Getting ready to go where?'

'I don't know,' said Kleber. 'Do you?'

Oh, yes, Elenya's death tore Kleber as when you tear a piece of paper in two, and yet he dreamed of people, how kind people could really be.

Loss, pity and love, thought Kleber: why is it that we all continue to sell the few things in our lives that we still understand? For don't you remember, he said to Elenya, the tender times we had together? And now look what fools our flesh has made of us all, and what's to be done about it?

'You must wait,' she said to him. 'We mustn't rush on each other again just yet. It would all be too sudden; such speed might lose us to each other.'

'I'm taking the first step into death, darling,' said Kleber. 'Tell me, is it cold?'

'Of course not,' she replied. 'Why would you want it to be cold?'

Kleber didn't see how he could go on putting up with the indifference of the people he saw around him on earth, and he began to sob on Elenya's half-forgotten words while she had still been with him. It was so bloody cold and dark in the street, considering his loneliness without her. He didn't want to know it ever again; anything was better than having to go through that again. The two of them had spoken about a great many matters during the little time they had had together, and now he found that he didn't know, knowing as much as he did through her, how he could really go on. The only crime he had ever committed was to fall in love, and so to understand another body, not seize it.

Oh, how crazy Kleber's grief was.

Further up the boulevard a man came up to Kleber and took him by the arm.

'You remember me?'

'Your face looks familiar,' said Kleber. 'Yes.'

'You did me a favour once. You got me off a major rap.'

'That's right,' said Kleber, 'so I did. It was back in 1981, wasn't it?'

'Yes. That wasn't my year,' said the man, 'though I had a good go at it.'

'Well, what's new?' said Kleber. 'Still on the bent side, are we?'

'How else could I make ends meet?'

'I don't know,' said Kleber, 'and, being busted, I frankly don't care.'

'I know all about that,' said the man. 'That's why I caught up with you. I know about your wife too.'

'Listen, do you know where my feller is?' said Kleber. 'Because I'm looking for him. Hard. You know. Extremely hard.'

'He's holed up in this district. I know that.'

'He would be,' said Kleber. 'He doesn't know any other hole. Except perhaps one other.'

'He's a shithead,' the man said, 'a real plank—even people like me don't like the cunt.'

'He's got every reason to look like a cunt,' said Kleber, 'because he is one, and will be for as long as he lives. Which won't be very long, because I'm patiently sealing him off from this city, from the centre of it that he depends on, and he'll soon have nothing but a dirty little hole to wait and crouch in until I reach him, and when I do reach him I'll kill him, and you can tell that to anyone you like.'

'I'm afraid I've got bad news for you,' the man said. 'I hate bringing it, but I was told to tell you.'

'More bad news? Is there any left? What is it?'

'It's about Mark.'

'What's the matter with him?'

'He's dead,' the man said, 'as dead as can be. That's what's the matter with him.'

'When? Tonight?'

'That's right. He was taken out in a car and shot on waste ground.'

'I see,' said Kleber. 'That does upset me. We were mates, you know. We went to school together.'

'I know.'

'The man I'm looking for over my wife: did he have a hand in it?'

'Yes. He had it done.'

'I really must get a medal done for the man and hang it on him personally,' Kleber said. 'It'll be a great pleasure, I can tell you.'

'I've got to go,' the man said. They nodded to each other in the rain, then the man turned down a side-street and disappeared.

He mourned Mark. He shouted out into the wet darkness.

Young tarts under their umbrellas watched him as he pounded his fists against his thighs and stamped off up the street. Kleber thought: The dead always speak first, and you just seemed to bleed away on them as if you were dying their deaths for them all over again, which seemed to him to be right—love for whom you loved, your debts all somehow paid, seemed to him to be the only way of living, though the glass in which you saw your image was terribly dark.

'You know, Elenya,' Kleber said.

'I'm here, darling.'

'I'm afraid of dying. It's not the pain I'm frightened of, but the change of state.'

'You mustn't be frightened, dearest, because, do you know, it hardly hurts at all.'

'Do you swear it? Because I feel that the first night of death must seem so strange.'

'It isn't like that, I promise you,' she said, 'and in any case I'm here waiting for you. You'll find that we shan't insist on keeping each other close, as we used to, not unless you need to. You'll just sleep and rest, have everything and everyone you need, so just be at ease.'

'I wouldn't tell anyone but you that I was afraid of dying.'

'I know.'

'What happened when you went up like that, in the car?' Kleber said.

'Car? Car?' she answered, puzzled.

'The thing you went up in.'

'Oh, yes,' she said, 'I remember. Oh, that? It was just one single burst of agony, a flash and it was over, and then it was now, here, where I am with you.'

'Protect me, darling,' Kleber said. 'I'm in great danger, Elenya. I'm alone without you and afraid.'

'But that's why I'm here,' she said, 'to protect you. I

can't be released until you are; and so I'm here to see you through.'

'Thank God.'

'You're right to thank him,' she said, 'because I know now that God is poor, sucked on and sought from.'

'So God's broke,' said Kleber, turning aside from her for an instant to mutter to himself. 'I knew it—robbed by his own servants.' He said to Elenya: 'What's a life truly worth?'

She said: 'You can't put a price on life.'

She left him for a while, and he kept going back meantime to the question that was central to him: what *was* a life truly worth? For he himself, with Elenya, had seen how sweet love could be, and the fact that he had just been demolished by its loss in no way changed his memories of it—no, the loss of her clarified them and he became more and more certain that, if he believed enough in the invisible, kicking aside the horrid little curtain that separated them both at present, their love, their arms, her body would all come pouring back.

And so, going on Sébastopol towards the Gare de l'Est, he continued his dialogue with her, stabbed through with his missing her.

For a little earlier on he had gone into his room at the *pension* to change his shirt and cook himself an egg, eat a piece of bread. He was crossing the room to the table when he saw just her hand lying across the back of the armchair. It was her very own hand, he saw at once, because he knew it as well as he knew his own; fine, pale, with those beautifully shaped nails she had; he had always particularly loved her strong, straight, well-shaped hands. The hand on the chair didn't move and he simply stood and stared at it intensely, his eggcup in one hand, the bread he had just cut in the other. He didn't dare go nearer to the hand in case he disturbed it; he didn't know what to do in front of the invisible become momentarily visible, where two worlds crossed—he was humbled and had to trust his instinct, which told him to stand still. It wasn't easy because of his eagerness to reach her, but he managed. He stared like a madman at the hand, observing that their wedding ring was no longer on its finger, but that there was still a pink mark on it where it had been before the ring was somehow lost in the explosion. He gradually digested the fact that there was just her hand. He also understood that her hand was present to give him hope of some kind. It was her left hand, the one he always automatically took in his when they went out into the street together, and the one that had been left perfect at her death. He knew that he mustn't speak and, standing there silently, he had a new and eternal vision of her, possible only through great suffering. He didn't know how long he stood there, motionless, dazzled; it could have been one minute or thirty. The hand suddenly became radiant, but softly so, in a way he couldn't describe, and he suddenly felt compelled to go towards her and press her fingers, as he saw them, against his lips. The time for him stood still for ever, and the next thing he knew was that the light in the room had changed and that his egg had gone cold. He couldn't eat it anyway and sat at the table, dreaming about her hand for about an hour, feeling so huge a longing for her that he wished he were dead to join her.

Kleber wasn't begging for mercy; he was pleading for it.

He couldn't understand yet, not really, that his wife and best friend were dead. Yes, he would change the whole face of the whole world with his tears, and the whole world would become his lost love. He himself had passed across the features of evil and been changed by them, so that in a way he knew everything. The evil had passed its fingers across Kleber's face, and his features had been changed by their touch and feel, but his love for Elenya was so strong that there was still something left of him. Love, too, had moulded his face; therefore he had been through the two great experiences on this earth and had nothing much else left to do. Evil had crossed it fingers in his face, and it had changed him from head to foot. In the past he had also often wondered why the people you loved themselves changed under a certain light as they turned, and how it was that their expressions changed as they moved from shadow to light, moving their heads, and yet altered all over again in their features with a hidden smile or sadness.

But that was all before. He had been only vaguely interested in the matter at the time, because it was before the impossible happened.

He remembered making love to other women long before Elenya: it was rather like a meeting at a busy station when you knew the other person had one eye on the clock.

He remembered how he had quarrelled with Elenya once. Only once: it was when he was late for a party, a lunch party, that she was giving for some friends of theirs. It hadn't really been Kleber's fault; he had been kept back on duty just at that moment when he was longing, as he always did, to get back to her. The single word she said to him was like a gun going off: she had loaded her mouth with it as if she had meant it to carry; of course she had learned how to do that on the street.

There had been nothing sentimental whatever in the

way that she had gone for him—fired at him, as it were, with her blazing face—nor in the way he had yelled back at her when she did it. Now he wrung his hands over this silly affair, but it had still been printed into him in the way you record a tape, and now he would have given anything to have played better music, but it was, of course, too late; so that now, now, now he didn't know what to do or where to turn, and he wasn't a weak man.

But now what could Kleber do but live out the hours of his life? He mourned the fact that he was even able to do it; he would have preferred to have been too stupid to be able to do it.

But as it was he asked himself: what can human beings expect of existence after all? One question, given the terms we live under, can be answered only by another question—in our life can there ever be a true answer?

15

He was out on Sébastopol again, walking through the rain towards the Gare de l'Est. He remembered some Shakespeare that he had studied for his English exams at school.

If you prick us, do we not bleed? He muttered the words aloud, and again passers-by turned to stare at him.

Just then, a woman came up and tapped his sleeve. He turned and saw it was a young prostitute.

'What is it?' he said. He didn't say it unkindly, but he didn't want to be interrupted in the course of his thinking just then: 'What do you want?'

'I want to talk to you,' she said. 'Please don't argue—I haven't much time. Follow me. This way. No, take my arm as if you were a client. That's better.'

'You know who I am,' said Kleber.

'Yes, that's why I'm here.'

'You'd best not be seen anywhere near me.'

'As if I cared.'

So then they turned off Sébastopol together, going to her place, she clacking along beside him in her miniskirt and red heels. For some reason, looking at her, he felt that he was on the point of understanding everything, all the infinite love and sadness in this world, instead of just the blindness and brutality. He imagined the trees he had seen at his grandparents' farm in the country, the poplars, swaying like bodies in love, a September wind, just before the leaves fell. He couldn't know what she was about to tell him, but then you could never know what life was about to tell you, no matter how logical you were. Anyway, too late he had discovered that love was every bit as tough as violence, and just as fatal.

Suddenly, Kleber could begin to see his bitterness—now he was a part of how intense human suffering could be. He didn't know why, walking beside her, he felt that; he just knew that he did. He understood that he had never really asked for anything much, yet he had a feeling inside him that he had demanded too much: he had asked for all love. He had got it all right, and then he had lost it, the only thing in life that could never be got back. Marching beside this girl he said aside to Elenya: 'I'm with you all the time. I hold you in my arms twenty-four hours a day. It's your voice, your body I bleed after, and the way you made our breakfast before I went to work; all the darkness that you turned into my light. Don't you remember how lovely you were that first summer we met, when we went down to the beach and you became so tanned and beautiful? Why did you die? Was it possible that you could die? You know you were my only treasure.' His loneliness and sorrow could never end now; even in the company of this other person, for which in a distant way he was grateful, his existence was finished; Elenya's loss cut into him wherever he looked or thought. The tragedy of existence, he now discovered, was that as you were on the point of living you were on the point of dying, and that when the greatest thing in your life died you, too, were dead. Afterwards others could only hold you gently by the wrist or forearm, get you a drink, joke to you, and beg you not to fall down and die.

'Do you know what love is?' Kleber said to the girl beside him.

'They say it's sweet agony,' she said, 'but I've never had

the experience.'

'I have,' said Kleber. 'I've learned about it in the worst of ways.'

'That's what I want to talk to you about,' the girl said.

'It wasn't as if I enjoyed murdering those three men,' said Kleber. 'You know about it?'

'Of course I do,' she said. 'Who doesn't? It was in the papers.'

'It was as if I were killing myself,' Kleber said, 'partly. I hated doing it. I did it to protect a friend.'

'I know you did.'

'You seem to know a good deal.'

'You could hardly live in this part of town otherwise, could you?'

'I love Paris,' said Kleber. 'It's my town, really, and I shall only get out of it dead.'

'Don't say that,' she said. 'You mustn't say that, you mustn't say things like that.'

'I'm dead already,' said Kleber, 'and I know it.'

'No.'

'It's life I love,' said Kleber, 'or I used to.'

'I try hard to hate it,' she said, 'but you can't really, can you?'

'Not in my case,' Kleber said, 'not even now.' The cigarette that he was smoking burned down steadily between his fingers as she held him by the arm.

'Suppose you were ill or mad,' she said, 'and I came to see you in hospital. Would you be glad?'

'If I were still in your world,' said Kleber, 'I would probably be the happiest man on earth if you did that. You can't really hate life, can you?'

'No,' she said, holding him tighter, 'only a good many things in it.'

'It's not our fault,' Kleber said. 'Not altogether, anyway.'

'I don't agree,' she said. 'It is. We let it happen the way it does.'

'I know,' said Kleber. She got in his way because he could only think about Elenya, and although this girl was trying to help he found he was thinking about Elenya in the only key he found possible: the key of infinite sadness.

'I fancy you quite,' she said.

'Do you?' said Kleber. 'I wish to God I felt the same but I don't.'

'No,' she said, 'you don't.'

'No,' he said. 'Not in view of what's happened to me.'

'Is it final?' she said seriously.

'It is, I'm afraid,' said Kleber, 'and I'm afraid of being afraid.'

'Don't be.'

'Worse luck, I've got to be. I'm so murderously sad that I can only listen to her and can't pay attention to you or anyone else.'

She held him tight by the hand and looked into his eyes: 'Don't die, will you? Above all, don't do that. Will you swear it?'

'I don't know what's going to happen now. No, I can't swear it.'

'What a bastard the street can be,' she said.

'It can be what it wants to be,' said Kleber, 'especially in this weather when it's pissing with rain. Yes, it can be rotten.'

'It's all right,' she said. 'Keep hold of me. Turn left here.'

He knew it was necessary to go with her, so they turned off the boulevard together arm in arm.

'We're here,' she said, stopping before an open doorway suffused with dark red light. They were going in when a thickset man in a black leather jacket and sneakers came up and said to the girl: 'Who's that?'

'It's all right,' the girl said. 'He's just a lonely man and his money's good.'

'It had better be,' said the man. He said to Kleber: 'I don't know you.'

'That's your bad luck,' said Kleber. 'Because I know you all right, flower; I didn't do a year with the vice squad for nothing.'

'I've placed you now,' said the man. 'You're that busted copper whose wife went up the spout. You're a walking disaster, I've heard.'

'Try not to be difficult,' said Kleber patiently. 'If you go on being so difficult, you'll regret it.'

'He's coming upstairs with me anyway,' the girl said to the man, 'and that's that, so get out of my way and fuck off.'

The man edged off at the way she said it but remarked: 'I might just see you afterwards, darling.'

'You might be doing a spell in hospital beforehand,' said Kleber. 'You know, before you get the chance to see anybody or do anything to them, OK? I'm one of those people who runs out of patience easily. I should just fade away if I were you.'

The man saw his meaning and did fade away.

'Well, come on up,' the girl said, and in the combined confusion of their limbs they walked up the worn-out stairs, as if madness and the spirit of living were suddenly mixed up—but what only Kleber knew was how terribly leaden he felt as he climbed. However, he said to her: 'It was a good thing your little fellow there went. He was in serious danger of looking like a cheap alarm clock run over by a lorry if he hadn't.'

'He's my pimp,' said the girl.

'I know.'

Derek Raymond

'I have trouble with people like that the whole time.'

'You would have in this job,' said Kleber. 'You know, you really ought to change it.'

'Where else could I earn money with the little brain I've got?' said the girl. 'Tell me that—it's easy to give advice that folk don't need, now be cool.'

'Yes, all right.'

She got hold of her keys and opened the door to her room. She switched on a light; the room was a strong pink colour, like roses. The partly open window filled the place with the noise of traffic, blocked out not far below by the rain and the usual quarrels in that narrow street.

'I've got to tell you something,' said Kleber. 'I don't really know why. I'm going to die in this city and it might be soon, very soon. You've got to die somewhere, of course, and I'd prefer to do it here.'

She started to weep, saying: 'Oh, Christ, what a fuck-up.'

'You mustn't cry like that. The state I'm in now, it really tears me apart.'

'I can't help it, I'm sorry.'

Later she sat on the bed, said *Ouf* and kicked her high heels off. 'I hate pimps,' she said.

'Who doesn't?' said Kleber.

'If you could fall in love with them it would be something, I suppose. But as it is they wouldn't give you the skin off their shit unless they could get a fiver out of it.'

He heard Elenya singing to him out of their past:

'Pick heavy yellow flowers for her,
When you're in love.

132

That smell of rain,
Sweet rain—
Yes, send her heavy flowers,
Heavy with your heart's pain…'

'Elenya must have talked about them.'

'Yes,' said Kleber. 'The memory doesn't make me feel any better. You knew her?'

'Yes,' said the girl, 'we worked together. We were good mates. My name's Tania, by the way.'

'I don't remember her ever mentioning you.'

'That must have been because once she was happy with you and you'd married her, she thought you wouldn't want to hear any more about all that.'

'That's right enough,' said Kleber. 'Listen, is this something about the man I'm after, the one who killed her?'

'Yes,' the girl said. 'Christ, when I heard about her death I nearly went mad, I tell you. She and I were really close.'

'What do you know?'

'You're not going to like it.'

'That doesn't matter,' said Kleber. 'I've got to hear it.'

'It's a nasty story.'

'I'm used to nasty stories.'

'Yes, but it's much worse when it's someone you love. Now you're here I'm beginning to wonder if I ought to tell you.'

'Tell it.'

'It happened six years back, well before you met her.'

There was a bang on the door and an old woman shouted: 'Shut up in there, will you? What the hell are you rambling on about, you little bitch? What's that you've got in there? A talking parrot?'

The girl screamed: 'Fuck off, you old bat, or I'll make a hole in you that's even bigger than your mouth is! I won't tell you twice.'

Kleber went over to her and ruffled her cropped hair in a rough yet tender way.

'His money had better be good,' the old woman yelled, 'because it'll be double price for the blag.'

'If you don't beat it, you old bag,' the girl screamed back, 'I'll pack up and leave in the morning and bang goes your fucking brothel because I'm half the age of all the other rats you've got in the place and I've twice the looks, so if you want to get hit in the handbag all you've got to do is rabbit on. You're making twice as much noise as we are anyway, you old slagheap, now shove it and go and wank yourself stupid!'

While he was sitting with Tania, the old woman banging on the door reminded Kleber of a time when he had been lying on the bed at the hotel and there was a little tapping on the door.

'Who is it?' said Kleber sharply, sitting up.

'It's me, darling.'

'But the door's open, I tell you. All you've got to do is come in, my sweet. The door's not locked.'

'I can't get in,' she said sadly.

'Come in! Come back, Elenya! Come back!'

'I can't.'

'Why?'

'It's too late.'

'Oh, for the love of God, angel, come to me.'

'No, I'm not allowed to.'

'Keep talking to me, Elenya, darling, I beg you. Don't go away.'

'People are calling me.'

'Oh, don't go, don't go, my sweet. Stay with me.'

'I'll come back. I'm always with you really. Where else could I be?'

'Elenya! Elenya!'

Silence.

'You've certainly got a tongue in your head,' Kleber was saying.

'Yes, and luckily a head to go with it,' the girl said. 'You've got to in this racket. I was an idiot ever to get into it, but you know what it is—you've got to live. I'll never get out again, except by a miracle, and as a copper you know that there aren't many of *them* about. Not around here, anyway.' She added inconsequentially: 'The trouble with these old buildings is that the walls are too thin. Everyone can hear every word you say, and it stops them fucking even if the man can get it up.'

Kleber was still thinking of Elenya, as he did all the time: 'My light, my sweetness. Come to me. Please come.'

'I'm here.'

'Well, he raped her,' Tania said. 'I know all about it for the simple reason that I was there.'

'Is there a washbasin anywhere around here?' said Kleber. 'I'm afraid I've got to be sick.'

'Behind the curtain over there.'

'Thanks.' He was frightfully sick, and it is one of the sounds that grief makes.

And so he tried to contemplate his vast loss.

Yesterday a letter from the bank had been sent to him at the hotel.

Kleber? he thought, reading his name on it, who was he?

I shall consider my death until I find it, he said to himself, and then perhaps I'll get Elenya back.

Tania spoke on but Kleber was still listening to Elenya through a few lines that a friend of his who fancied himself as a poet had written, as many young mad boys do, but which had touched him then and since—otherwise why did he remember them now:

> 'Give me a pinprick somewhere simple,
> And not a heartache till the summer ends…'

Yet he thought of Tania: how sweet people really are, not like some cunts. He also thought, calculating silently: I'm forty—it's taken me fourteen thousand, six hundred days to become any kind of human being at all, and I still somehow haven't understood anything.

He nodded gravely at Tania from that other world where he was now, for ever on his own in his sorrow and his love. What he really would have wanted, if only it had been possible, would be to love everybody on earth—but, of course, it was much too late for such an existence now, as all vital matters always are. Nor could he manage to understand how he had been so ordinary up until Elenya's death, which had robbed him of his dullness just as love does, both being final. For some reason it was the year 1600 all over again. It was always that year for Kleber now, and he was beginning to believe that despite appearances it always had been so for him, and that perhaps he might even have lived and died yet again in that time. The unimaginable pain of human existence was right now for Kleber: tonight and now. He knew objectively that he was undergoing the most terrible suffering: his body was being played out through the key of sadness. He glanced at himself in Tania's small mirror and saw not a face but only something that wanted to die. His eyes glittered darkly back at him; they were no longer ordinary eyes. He observed with them that he had been forced out of ordinariness by events. He wiped the last of his vomit away from his mouth with a red towel he found and went to look out of the window while Tania went on speaking. He watched the unending rain that came down harder than ever; there was enough water in the sky for anyone's destruction. He stood listening for Elenya, longing for her to come, but there was nothing to be heard or seen but the night, the traffic, voices and the rain. It seemed to him almost as though there were no more people for him—not real people—and there was the paradox, for he was so filled up with love for them that it had spilled over.

Ideas and feelings raced through him as he rested his grieving head against the window, which he had opened, out into the wet air of our life; for now he understood what love really is. Something so obvious and pure that all he had to do was stay the same, so as to be able to take love properly into his arms where it belonged, though most people would never understand. No, for except sometimes in their dreams too many people would never realise how love responds; Kleber knew that now. Kleber knew everything now, but what was the use of his knowledge when it was no longer worth him knowing it? He thought back to the days when he and Elenya had been so happy through some universal language of their blood—even now he was still, somewhere inside him, running excitedly along a street to meet her, and everything he had ever known or felt was all still so new and yet so terribly wrinkled and old.

Kleber said to himself, staring outdoors: What do I look like to the other? Where is the other? Give the other to me, and I shall become the other.

He was filled with intolerable sadness and love, and realised now that he had never really been a policeman at all.

Not *really*. Not in his reality.

He remembered how as a child in his village his family had described to him how life had been a matter of birth, then the pains of youth, and then love, marriage, years of work and at last death. Thinking of this, all the sweetness and tears in his blood arose. For in villages people were good because they were true. All Kleber wanted to know now was: to what extent is it possible for just one person to know and suffer? And why?

He wanted to know: why must people for ever buy and sell each other?

Why was it that one's life question put to the life of another could never have any real answer? I'm destroying myself, he thought, but for others. All the others will somehow save me, I know, just as the villagers did for each other, both through love and necessity, in the old days. It was all so difficult and so obvious to him now.

'The man took us both back to the place he had at the time,' Tania was saying, 'with three of his men. They were all bastards. He had plenty of money on him, but, of course, he wouldn't give us any of it until we'd performed. It's one of those cases, you know, where you just shut your eyes and let it happen—because it was all what we think of as clear money, down to us, no one to pay off.'

'Go on.'

'Well, right away, in the sitting room, he started manhandling Elenya. I was supposed to go off with the other three, but I wouldn't leave Elenya because I was worried about her.'

'What do you mean, manhandling?'

'I mean rape.'

Kleber wrote his own epitaph and turned his head aside to his grave when he heard that. Like Robespierre's, his epitaph consisted of one word: 'sleep!'

'It happened right there, in his sitting room,' Tania continued. 'I tell you, I was meant for the other three, and they tried to force me into a bedroom with them, but I wouldn't go. So things turned ugly—you know what I mean?'

'All too well.'

'Well, Elenya was patient—she didn't turn violent or anything silly like that but kept her head and tried to talk him down, you know, but then he suddenly got hold of her by the front of her dress and simply ripped it off her. I said to the fat cunt, I'll scream if you do any more to her, and he said, scream all you like, darling—there's no one to hear you but me, and as a matter of fact I happen to love it when women scream. As far as I'm concerned they only exist to give my prick something to think about—it's better than wanking, and you can think yourself fucking lucky that it's her I want and not you; otherwise you'd suffer, I can tell you.'

Kleber felt as if his whole head was coming away from his eyes, and he watched death waltzing towards him while his skull felt like an empty dance hall with a little mad music playing in it. Tania reached over, touched him on his arm and said in a low voice: 'I'm sorry. Perhaps I shouldn't have told you any of this, but I believed I had to. Do you want me to go on?'

'Yes,' said Kleber.

'The others tried to get me away so I couldn't watch, but I clung to the sofa and screamed while he threw her on the floor, and then when he saw how her legs were twisted around each other and would never open for him he put the boot in and kicked her black and blue. He missed her left eye by less than an inch; then he picked her up with the strength they have when they're in that state and smashed her face into the wall while the others held me down with their hands across my mouth to stop me yelling. At last he turned to his men, grinning at them across her unconscious head, and said, that's all right, I can have her now. I like them like that, raw meat—I've thought about her for months, that pretty little Polish tart. I said, she was pretty until you started on her, you fat bastard. You shut your face, you slut, he said, or I'll give you a hammering as well. I love it, that's how I get my rocks off, only I don't fancy you, so why don't you just fuck off? But I wouldn't; I only clung to the sofa with all my might. God, what a horrible room—like a well-lit torture chamber, its walls plastered with what villains think of as art. The minute I got a chance, I picked up a pink vase and threw it at him but it missed and broke the mirror behind him. You little cow, he said, I'll see to you, but right now I've got something else on, like a hard-on. He managed to get his pants down as far as his ankles and there was his huge prick half up, inclined to the left with a purple top to it, it was quite disgusting, and in it went into her, I'm afraid, but she couldn't have known much about it, I don't think, if that's any comfort to you.'

'It isn't,' said Kleber. (He repeated to himself: Kleber? Who was he? What was he for?) He said:'Well? How did it end up, this marvellous party?'

'The others went through me, and then when they'd all had enough they threw us out on to the street with a warning not to say anything to anyone. And we didn't, because the bastard's powerful on Sébastopol, as you well know.'

'You're right,' said Kleber. (He had noticed the scar at the corner of Elenya's eye but for some reason had never questioned her about it. He saw now that the reason must have been instinct.) He went over to the window again and stared out at the night. Would morning never come?

'It will come,' Elenya answered.

He said to Tania: 'What did you do about Elenya?'

'I took her to hospital, of course. We saw a young doctor and I told him some story about a street accident. He didn't believe it, but that didn't matter; he was on our side anyway. Don't worry, he said to me, we'll look after her, and there won't be any questions, I'll see to that.'

'I must go and thank him,' said Kleber. 'How long was Elenya in hospital?'

'Ten days—and I can tell you, she needed to be.'

'I can see that,' said Kleber. He stood up. 'It's much better that all this has come out. Well, thank you.'

'I hope you'll be all right,' she said. 'Be careful.'

But Kleber was already on his way downstairs.

*

141

He felt like marble after what he had just heard. He didn't feel close to tears, even; he no longer felt close to anything human. He just walked slowly on up Sébastopol like an automaton. What a brave darling you were, he kept saying to himself, what a brave, brave girl, no wonder I loved you so much. He found he was telling himself a story as he walked: one day in paradise, God said to his angels, I'm old and tired; go down into the world for me and see if you can find any pity in it: pity must be found. All but one came back and said there was none, but one stayed and died again and so became pity. Now that dead angel was whispering in Kleber's ear and Elenya said just two words: 'Darling. Darling.' He burst out crying, and people looked closely at him as they passed.

He walked on in the drowning rain, through dead leaves flying on the wind and past the shuttered fronts of bars, feeling as if his throat were made of stone.

He was relieved that he had kept calm in front of Tania just now; he didn't quite know how he had done it.

'Elenya! Elenya! Elenya!' he shouted. 'Come back! Speak to me, for the love of God!'

But there was no answer for him but the whisper of the pitiless rain.

So on and on he went in the dark.

Some time later he tried to use his reason, but he found that reason, in his situation, was of no more use to him than if he had been on his deathbed. So finally he gave it up and said to himself: if I can't escape my end by logic, what can I do, since logic merely confirms that there is only one end?

Perhaps he could go mad after all, he said to himself. He could see himself stumbling after a barrow of weeds along the paths of some country asylum, a barrow whose handles he was holding with hands that seemed not to be his own, and he realised what he had always known: that he could never go mad.

So that was why Kleber found that he was crossing over into another world, having been driven out of this one by grief, and it was why he thought: I must bring all this to an end and find Elenya again, because I would rather be nothing than endure this separation. I still hope, he said to himself: I must keep hoping, even though despair's the fashion. He saw now, far too late, that for too long his principal love had been his love of himself, and he was now trying to make amends to Elenya by final, appalling efforts, efforts to get back to the surface; he felt as a man does when he is trapped deep under the ocean.

Suddenly he smelled dead chrysanthemums and knew that there wouldn't be long to wait; he would be with her even before her funeral.

What such loss did was make you lose your identity, and then nothing really mattered any more: and such is fate, human misery and death.

16

Kleber was remembering, as he walked, how when he was ten or so he had once spent a week at his grandmother's farm. The others—his parents, his widowed grandmother—were out in the fields while he, seized by a spirit of adventure, ran back into the house. After going through its labyrinth of rooms he found himself in front of a heavy door. He stood facing it for a moment, then grasped the handle, turned it and forced the door creaking back into the room. The room was dark, even though the shutters were open, even though it was a fine summer's day in July, and even though the room had once been painted white. What struck him at once was how cold it was in there—also the dank smell of disuse and the pictures that spiders had knitted to the walls. Laboriously, he pushed the door to behind him and shivered—not from fear but from the chill in there after the heat outside. He studied the pictures (they were old photographs, faded ones) with all the attention that children have at that age. Even though he wasn't old enough to understand what he was seeing, he still absorbed it all: there were four photographs, all of men, and from the fixed stare that each of them had he understood that they had been dead even before they had died. He could see from their clothes that they were from another age, and had been dead for a long while. They were heavy, working men, dressed for some occasion in their Sunday best. But it was the expression in the eyes of all of them that struck him; it was their

145

destiny they were facing, not the camera. Judging by the
dust in the room it must have been decades since it was
swept and cleaned, and he knew by instinct that nobody
ever went in there. Such furniture as there was (three
chairs, an old divan pushed into a corner, a table with
one broken leg propped up on a brick) was rotten and
perished; flies and bees hissed, rattled and muttered
against the cracked window. It was darker in there, he
felt, than it should have been at four o'clock on a hot
afternoon. Even the insects didn't like it; it was a psychic
darkness.

Then the door groaned open suddenly and his
grandmother shrieked, 'You! What are you doing in
here! Get out at once!' and she gave him a terrible
smack. He recalled that he had burst out crying, not
from the blow but because of the contrast with the other
world inside the room. He went to his mother later and
asked her: 'Why oughtn't I to have gone into the room?'

And his mother whispered: 'Ssh, because it's unlucky—
no one ever goes in there, it's the room of the dead. Did
you see the photographs of the men?'

'Yes. Who were they?'

'Your grandmother's brothers. Three of them hanged
themselves here for no reason, and the fourth was shot
for cowardice after the Chemin des Dames. After that
the room was never opened again. They had used it to
kill themselves and died what the family considered to
be dishonourable deaths, so the room was locked up by
your grandfather.'

'But it wasn't locked. The door yielded quite easily to
me.'

'I don't understand,' his mother said. 'It's always locked.'

'Well, it wasn't. And, anyway, I don't think you can lock
the past away with a key.'

'The trouble with you is that you think too much,' his mother said, 'you're far too independent-minded for a boy of your age—now go to bed.' She added: 'Weren't you afraid in there?'

'No. Just very sad.'

'I don't know what's going to become of you in life,' his mother said, 'but going into that room won't bring you any luck.'

Why should he be thinking of all that now, at such a moment as this, walking up Sébastopol in the rain? But there it was, as clear as yesterday.

I don't know what's going to become of you in life, his mother had said. Well, now he knew, all right. A thought came to him: I believe I've been frightened so often in my life that I no longer know any more what fear means—all I understand now is pain and loss. You end by being rendered down by the sheer passage of time, and your living time goes back to the purity of gold in a river—back to a wilderness of stone discovered in a barrow after thousands of years.

'Why?' said Kleber aloud. 'There is no why. And if there's no why, there's no where.' He knew this thinking to be the policy of disaster, yet he wouldn't give up hope even now—not after hearing Elenya's voice, not after seeing her hand on the back of the chair, the long white fingers that had so often caressed his body, the bright, beautiful manicured nails, and the slight flexing movements of the fingers that he knew so well. She had entered the world by means of a depraved parent, her father, and had endured constant moves with a series of battered suitcases thrown into half-wrecked vans from one dull quarter of the suburbs to another—and then she had been forced on to the streets to undergo the kind of horror that Tania had just related to him.

Yet innocence had surged up in her again the minute she first met Kleber.

And so, thinking of these things, Kleber's throat broke up from marble into water as he stamped up the vast street with his head down in case anyone should see his eyes.

'I'll see you all off, you bastards,' he said. 'As long as I live, it may take me five minutes or fifty years, but I'll do it, you'll see. Bloodshed is bloodshed and you'll pay for it—I never let go.'

And so Kleber walked on up the street.

At last Kleber found himself at the end of Sébastopol, very near to the Gare du Nord. He walked through on to the main concourse of the station as if in a dream— for he had no good reason to be there. He watched the great trains come and go, listening to the electronic bells of imminent departures for Brussels, Antwerp, Amsterdam and Oslo: even Warsaw, if you went far enough. The concourse was thick with people intent on adventures meaningless to anyone but themselves: each one a tiny insect intact in itself, spinning out the secret web of its life in a corner that not even its prey or partner could ever share. He watched them and ticked them off with the eyes that any long-service copper has—but none of that had anything to do with what was going on behind his face. The hands of the station clock struggled around the lighted dial above him—the short one hopelessly pursuing the long one (or was it the other way around?) like a greyhound pursuing an electric hare in a race reduced to the slowest possible motion. Women towing suitcases on wheels, businessmen in macintoshes carrying briefcases, old peasants leaning on the sticks of illness (where did you serve, Kleber wondered) passed in front of him—also Arabs, Turks, Moroccans in long striped gowns and round hats, quite a few of whom Kleber recognised, for he had arrested them in his early days for cheating foreign tourists, who couldn't speak a word of French, out of their money. He stared hard at one or two of them as if he were still working, and they knew that he saw them, and why he saw them. Or they thought they knew; in fact he wasn't really looking at them at all, but at his own catastrophe.

A mob of students in anoraks stormed past him gabbling in German with kitbags on their shoulders, and that was when Kleber heard tears behind him and turned sharply. He knew the sound of tears and suffering if anyone did and went straight up to the child and took her by the arm; she was about fourteen.

'What's the matter, darling?'

She was in a state of panic, but at last she managed to explain that she had lost her parents at the station, and that she was stranded without any money.

'Will you come with me?' said Kleber.

'Only if you swear not to harm me.'

'That's easy for me to swear,' Kleber said, 'and I swear it.'

So they went to the stationmaster's office and the clerk said: 'What do you want?'

'I don't want anything,' said Kleber, 'but this girl's lost her parents and she's upset.'

'Look,' said the clerk, 'this station is a very busy place.'

'I can see it is,' said Kleber, 'so let's have some real action in it, shall we?'

'Listen,' said the clerk, 'why don't you just call the police? That sort of thing's their job.'

'Human distress is always somebody else's job,' said Kleber. 'It's a funny thing about the world we all live in, haven't you noticed?'

'I mean, *I* don't know what's happened to this kid's parents. Why should I?'

'No reason,' said Kleber.

'Normally I'd do something,' said the clerk, 'only it's tricky right now, see, because we're in a state of industrial action here at the moment.'

'I see,' said Kleber. 'So on account of that this child can wander around Paris without a penny in her pocket, get raped, run over or killed. Is that it?'

'I hadn't thought of it quite like that,' said the clerk, 'but broadly I suppose that's what it might come down to, yes. It's the union that gives me my orders, so I'm sorry—while industrial action is on there's nothing I can do about the child or anything else much.'

'I wonder what you'd do if it were your own daughter,' Kleber said. 'I'm glad you're not this one's father, I can tell you that. Good night.'

When they got outside the girl said to him: 'What are you going to do now?'

'Get a cab to my place,' said Kleber. 'What's your name?'

'Sophie.'

So they went out into the street to find a taxi.

Kleber opened the door of his hotel room and they went in.

'Sit down,' said Kleber. 'How about a cup of tea? It's about all there is, I'm afraid, though we could go out and have supper if you feel hungry.'

'No, just some chips might be nice in a while,' she said,

'but meantime do you mind if I chew gum?'

'Certainly not,' said Kleber, 'though I'd have thought it would taste funny with tea.'

'No, they go fine together.'

'Feeling better?'

'Yes,' she said, 'but it's you I'm worried about; you don't look good to me.'

'Oh, I'm all right.'

'No you aren't,' said Sophie.

'All right,' said Kleber. 'Well, I'll tell you straight out then—something so dreadful's just happened to me that I don't know what to do about it.'

'I might be able to help,' said Sophie, 'you never know.'

'We ought to sort out your problems with your parents first.'

'They can wait,' said Sophie. 'After all, they made me wait. Now come on. Talk if you feel you can.'

'Well, I want to talk,' said Kleber, 'only I'm in such a bad state that I don't know how to start. Anyway, it's like this—my wife was killed yesterday morning and I loved her so much that now I want to die because I can't get used to her loss.'

Sophie put her hands out and took him by the wrists. 'How did it happen?'

'I'm a busted copper who helped out an old friend of mine in the mob,' he said, 'and Elenya was blown to bits by a bomb planted in a car that was intended for me.'

'Look,' said Sophie, 'wherever she is now, as long as she somehow knows you still love her, and always think of her and never forget her, it's not quite so bad.'

'You're a real little lady,' said Kleber, 'but my grief is where it will always be. We were only married four years, but we felt completely together, that's all I can say.'

'Then I'm sure your love will carry on for ever,' said

Sophie, 'if your love was true.'

'Thank you,' said Kleber. 'Thank you so much for what you've said. Let's talk about you now. Why were you crying there at the station?'

'Ah, that was despair,' she said. 'The same thing happens with my parents over and over when they promised it wouldn't. We were all going to Belgium on holiday, and then they have to quarrel again, both of them drunk, and they leave me with no money, no ticket, nothing—not even a key to our flat so that I could get back in.'

'I'll bet they'll have sobered up by now and be worried about you,' said Kleber. 'We'll do something about it straight away.' He got his money out of his back pocket. 'Now look—I don't want any argument about it—take this. Here's five hundred francs, Sophie, and if that doesn't turn out to be enough you can leave a message downstairs here any time—so take it.'

'Don't I have to do anything for it?' she said warily.

'Nothing but put it in your pocket,' Kleber said. 'I don't buy and sell people.'

'Tell me,' said Sophie, 'do you believe that there was once a time, long ago, when people were innocent?'

'They say there was.'

'And are you yourself convinced?'

'I am,' Kleber answered slowly. 'People died in droves to save us, you know.'

'I'm too young to remember.'

'We both are,' said Kleber, 'but the people who fought did it out of conviction and died horribly so that you and I could be here now, having this conversation in this room. And now I'm going to get you back to your parents.'

'Suppose I didn't want to go back to them?'

'You must,' said Kleber.

'Can't I stay here?'

'No,' said Kleber. 'I'm in a terrible situation which I can only resolve by myself. For their sakes, I don't want anybody else dragged into it. You've got to understand that, Sophie.' He picked up the telephone and called his old police station. He said to the man on duty: 'You know who it is.'

'Yes,' said the man, 'get off the line.'

'Listen,' said Kleber, 'I've got a kid with me, she's only fourteen, she's lost her parents, she's lost her parents at the Gare de l'Est, so forget the rules for a minute—I found her in tears going up and down the platforms without a penny. So get down here fast and collect her. It's the Hôtel du Bourg, off the Boulevard de Sébastopol, Room 41, do it fast; I hope for your sake you're here in ten minutes.'

He hung up and said to Sophie: 'They're coming down for you now and they'll help you find your people, so don't get in a state over it.'

'If I'm in a state,' the girl said, 'it's not over me, it's over you.'

'That's a very sweet thing to say,' said Kleber, 'and I'll remember it. But don't you bother about me: I always manage.'

'Christ, I hope you do,' she said seriously, 'seeing what's already happened to you. But in any case, I'll never forget tonight.'

'There'll always be people around to look after a girl like you,' said Kleber; 'yes, to look after someone like you.'

'Not many,' she said.

'No, but there'll be some,' he said. 'There'll always be some; enough.'

She suddenly ran at him and threw her arms around

him and said: 'You're lovely.'

'That's not what everyone thinks,' Kleber said.

'I don't care what everyone thinks,' the girl said. 'As a matter of fact I don't care what anyone thinks.'

That was when they heard the usual kind of tread the law has on the stairs, and Kleber went over to the door to let them in.

The two brand-new uniformed Sherlocks who stuck their noses in didn't pay the least attention to Kleber, but instead sailed straight into the girl in a menacing way as if she'd raped someone or something. The one who was really stupid, the one who never let his face muscles move, said: 'OK, darling, what's all this down to, then? Let's have it.'

Kleber leaned against the wall with his arms crossed and watched them, amused.

The thinner of the two turnips, the one who thought he was clever, perhaps because he had a long nose, said to her: 'Did a certain person present in this room proposition you in any way? Make advances? Any slap or tickle at all?'

'No,' said the girl, showing him the five-hundred-franc note. 'All he slapped me with was this, and you can check that the ink's dry on it.' She added: 'You can double it, if you like. There's a man in this room,' she added dreamily, 'and do you know that I believe he's the only man in here?'

It took the pair of them a good minute to work that out, and before they had quite managed it the girl said: 'I'm sorry he's not my father or brother, that's all, this man you seem not to want to talk to.'

There was a silence after that and then the long-nosed copper said: 'OK, we'll go over the whole lot down at the station. Come on.'

So she picked up her coat and bag.

'Mind how you go, love,' Kleber said. 'Now take care.'

It seemed to him that she smiled at him for a very long time but it can only have been for the moment that it took her to cross the room, and then she was gone for ever, Kleber staring down at her as she crossed the pavement to get into the police car. As the door slammed, he turned back into his darkening room, more alone, he felt, than ever: but then suddenly Elenya was with him, her arm around him, saying: 'Try to understand what's happening to you now, because you're being transformed and crystallised, although the way it all has to be done still seems to you to be infinitely complex. And I mean infinitely complex, because you're about to be liberated, my darling, my sweet prince, and that's going to mean that there'll no longer be any wall between us; we shall never ever have to fight against any wall again, so that there won't be any further death to separate us, never, never, never—for the true meaning of space is that space has no true meaning, so that truly there is no space. I was seized with so vast a joy when you found that child at the station, and in the way you found her, for I was just beside you as I always am, and it was the same as if the child were the child that you and I never had the time to have. For you know that in spite of everything that has happened, I am always in your arms and that I hold you; for even absence has an end.'

'But how long, how long?' Kleber whispered.

'Ah, time, time,' she answered sadly. 'For as long as you exist on earth you keep worrying about time just as I once did when we were both together. But now you are between two banks of a river to get to the further bank and I know how you're struggling in the water, darling, and how dark and deep it is; that last battle is too slow

Derek Raymond

for you. But I *am*. I exist without time. Where I am now there's no more space; no time and no pain. And if it's the second of death you're afraid of I hereby abolish it with my arms. Only, my sweetheart, listen to me onwards until the end, for it's you who holds the power for both of us now.'

He felt her leaving him and screamed: 'Oh, Christ, take all our pain in your hands and break its neck for us!' And he visualised Elenya until he could see her behind the blackness of his closed eyes and said: 'Oh, let me plunge into your dark splendour; that's all I long for now, darling.'

He remembered how, only three months earlier, it was his weekend off and he and Elenya had gone to see her cousin in a country asylum. He had been there, or in places like it, since he had been a child of two, because of a fall he had had on a flight of stairs. Now he was thirty-six, and Kleber saw him this minute as he always would, watching him and Elenya without making the slightest noise over an absent smile, holding a toy lorry loosely in his right hand. When Kleber saw how huge the bones of his shoulders were, fleshless under the worn, ill-fitting tweed, he wanted to say something that would somehow make everything all right; but his lips were stiff and white, he found, and stayed silent. They approached with the bag of sweets and the new clothes they had brought him, but the sick man didn't touch them; he just stood politely in his world now that they had given him so many drugs to take his violence away.

The male nurse seemed to Kleber to be as intelligent a witness as anyone could have, so he took him aside on an impulse and said, 'What's really left of him?' whereon the male nurse answered, 'Not much, but he's nice and quiet, isn't he?'

'He certainly doesn't move at all,' said Kleber. 'Can he?'

'Only if you guide him,' said the male nurse, 'then he'll smile and come with you as willing as a horse.'

'What about his teeth?' Elenya said, turning to the nurse.

'Oh, that worked fine,' said the nurse. He explained for Kleber's sake: 'We had to remove fourteen of them together—the dentist doesn't care to come up here every day, and his teeth were all rotten. It's because he can't work in the garden so he never has any appetite, but, of course, we make sure he gets all the protein and vitamins he needs.'

Kleber remembered asking himself what the use of it all was: wouldn't the sick man be better off dead?

It burned him now to think back to the way Elenya had stroked the great hole, three centimetres in diameter, at the right-hand base of her cousin's head.

She was the only one who ever came to see him, and he could see her now; she stroked his head the way that lovers do, her fingers soft, subtle, random and also intense as they touched his skull where he had hit the stairs when he fell. Elenya said to Kleber, 'I'm sure he knows more than he can say,' and Kleber answered, 'Yes, probably.'

'Isn't he giving us a nice smile?' said the nurse. 'My, he seems happy today.'

'What happens when he isn't?'

'Oh, nothing. He just goes dark.'

The only trouble with the smile was that it never varied. 'Can I speak out right in front of him?' Kleber said.

'Oh, certainly,' the nurse said. 'If he does understand us

it'll only be in his own way, and nobody can know what that is.'

Kleber looked at the sick man, smiling with his toy held loosely in his hand, dressed in his tweed jacket, denim trousers and heavy peasant boots, a clean check shirt. He gazed at them, through them and past them.

'What I admire about you,' Kleber said to the nurse, 'is the way you keep him so neat and clean.'

'Yes, but that's our job.'

'Not a hundred years ago he'd have been lying on a bed of straw with people peeping at him through a barred door.'

'At least we've managed to change that.'

'Yes,' said Kleber. 'Thank God and well done'—for he knew that he himself would never have had the courage and selflessness to work year in, year out at such a job as that in such a place. Now several other insane people, all men, most of them old, blotted out in their world, gathered around the door at the sound of normal voices. None of them spoke, but they looked at Kleber and Elenya from eyes at the point where they had been annihilated. Kleber, disturbed, went to look out of the ground-floor window; in the garden an old man was playing a curious game with himself, stealing and peering through the trees and bushes. He was a peasant, and parted the branches carefully with a stick he had, and then moved off secretly to another bush, taking great care over the manoeuvre, stalking very slowly in his slippers to a different part with a graven face whose expression never changed.

'He looks as if he knows something we don't,' Kleber said to the nurse.

'I agree—but the trouble is, we don't know what it is because they can't tell us.'

'What a terrible place this world really is,' said Kleber.

'You shouldn't worry about it as much as you do,' said the nurse.

'In my job,' said Kleber, 'there's not much else you can do. It's that—or not worry at all.'

'They don't live in our world.'

Yes, but to Kleber this seemed to make everything worse, because these people were so vulnerable, and he was powerless to help them. The experience struck him hard because, unlike Elenya, who had often been to visit her cousin, Kleber had never been in such a place before and found himself stirred by pity, horror and grief of which he had never previously known himself capable.

When it was time for them to leave, with the evening shadows stealing over the garden, which meant suppertime for them, Kleber put his hand on the shoulder of the sick man who never moved but smiled on at him and said: 'Goodbye. Hold up, old man. We'll meet again.'

When they got out to their car, he and Elenya stood for a while together silently, hand in hand on the gravel path. After Paris, it was quiet and peaceful down there in the country—gentle, rolling land, with a twelfth-century church in the middle distance.

You shouldn't worry as much as you do, the nurse had said, but Kleber did worry. He worried because he wanted to be told why it was that they didn't treat the sane as well as they did the man—he was thinking of the people he had to arrest, of course, who were put through hell in another but equally special way. After all, in his job, he helped control it all, if that was the word for it.

It took him at least an hour to adjust to his and Elenya's own world once they had passed through the gate of the asylum, and, as he always did, he told her so. There were never any secrets between them. While they drove he told her every single thing he had felt while they were there. She comforted him with her words; she always did. She took his hand in hers and squeezed it.

For Kleber, as he drove, the mad went on trotting at the handles of the barrows of vegetables on great in-turned feet to the gardens behind the asylum, or else to the kitchens, coming and going and whispering to themselves. He could see them as clear as pictures, and it was more painful than any music.

'What we want to do for them,' the nurse had said to them both as they left, 'is to give them back the dignity they're entitled to, don't you see?'

How did you manage to love everybody if you were just an ordinary poor cunt? Now he was already beginning to know, driving with Elenya. You managed to love everybody through loving somebody.

(The mad went trotting on, trailing their spades and hoes into the gardens behind the asylum; the bees hummed among the tomato plants and things, carefully tended, grew, were reaped and died, as all things must.)

'For all suffering is fatal to us,' Elenya whispered to him now. 'And we both know it, for the two of us are being transformed.'

Now Kleber was beginning to have some idea of what being at the front of some stupid war and advancing under fire really meant, where there was no cover. He was on fire with rage. For it was the great Perseus who returned to say, after his own battle, that there was no looking the Medusa in the face—she was too evil, she was evil itself, and could only be obliquely destroyed by means of the mirror made by a burnished shield.

Nothing had changed. The faster time runs out for me, thought Kleber, the vaster I see the questions are that have to be opened. I see everything now; but what's the use of that when it dies with me? Now, through Elenya's death, I understand what the New Testament really meant. Christ, our Passover is sacrificed for us—it means that we too must pass over as she has. I was too obstinate and stupid to see the truth before, but it's horribly simple: you live and die for the position you've decided to hold.

It was why, long before the arrival of Elenya in his life, Kleber had always been afraid of love; it was why he had always insisted with himself and others that he was so hard, when he was not. It was the loss of love that frightened him far more than death itself. As for himself and the others who directly and indirectly had been responsible for Elenya's death, what was frankly rotten, frankly stank. Kleber thought: let the others munch their oranges in the stalls and watch our tragic spectacle, she and I, while they tumble about laughing, drink and remember their shopping.

In the middle of Paris, now, it was always the year 1600 for Kleber.

He was being driven mad by life driving him out of life itself because of Elenya's death, and so he was willing to destroy himself, and destroy others, out of grief; it was all a dead love story in the street.

He half-dreamed as he stumbled along Sébastopol of some sleeping prince on a castle wall.

Kleber wished he could fall into some deathly sleep but knew that he could not, not yet.

17

Kleber found himself in another bar. He ordered a kir and asked the barman the usual question: 'Have you seen my man?'

'No, I haven't. Now look. I'll serve you, OK? As long as you keep your fucking mouth shut.'

'That's all right,' said Kleber, 'as long as you make sure he gets the message, because I know he likes coming in here. It's almost like a kind of vendetta. It's all about my wife, you know. I want to thank the man warmly over my wife.'

'Just keep quiet,' said the barman. 'I'm warning you.'

Kleber got up from the bar, went out into the street and was terribly sick. As he slowly recovered, he wondered whether it would ever be necessary for him or anybody else ever to go through such suffering again, or whether his own agony could ever end. Vomiting the last of his stomach out, he tried to empty himself of all the dark, filthy music that filled his soul.

Evil and loneliness—they were the dead sisters, whispering hand in hand through the night of men.

'What was that?' said the barman. 'Repeat that. I didn't like the sound of it.'

Kleber had no idea he had spoken aloud. But he repeated it—at least as well as he could remember it.

'Fuck off out of here,' the barman said. 'I warned you.'

'What about Mark?' said Kleber. 'The night I watched him lend you two hundred francs? You wept with relief over him, but now he's riddled with bullets you'll never have to pay him back.'

'I keep telling you to get out of here; otherwise I'll call the law.'

'I'm a distracted man,' said Kleber. 'Call the law. I used to be it.'

'You're not any more,' said the barman. 'Now get out of here. It's your last chance.'

'I know what you mean,' said Kleber. He got up and left. He went back to his hotel room, walking slowly, as the dawn rose over all the trouble in the world. The state he was in, it wasn't easy for him to think, yet there were moments like now when thinking seemed desperately necessary to him. It didn't do any real good yet seemed to help him just as the very idea of water helps to force you through a desert. Thinking was like a compass of some sort to him in his nightmare—it seemed to stabilise him in his disaster.

'Oh, speak to me, Elenya. I need you, but I can't feel you now.'

But there was no answer for him, and Kleber saw how only great love could ever breed such despair.

When he was back in his room, Elenya was suddenly present and said: 'You're faint, darling, you're worn out—come close to me, no, closer, lean down here on my breast, which was only ever for you.' It was very dark in the room.

'When did I start to go into the dark, darling?' said Kleber. 'When I went into that room? When I fell in love with you?'

'You were destined for the dark,' she said, 'my sweet, my sweet heart's blood.'

When she was with him they could talk about

anything now.

'Can you feel my body?' he implored her.

'Oh, very nearly. I almost can. For you remember: I *gave* mine to you, and never seized it.'

'Stop! Stop!' he shouted.

Her presence was as painful as her absence.

'Ssh,' she whispered. 'You don't know as much as I do now: be comforted by my nearness to you and you won't grieve nearly so much.'

Listening to her words and feeling her so warm and close to him as he lay on the bed, Kleber suddenly thought about Elenya's idiot cousin. 'Somebody has to suffer and die for us, I suppose,' he said, 'but why?'

'Don't ask,' she said, 'you'll send me away with your questions. Accept it all as it is. Here where I am I swear to you it's all light, and you have your special place waiting for you among us. I shall be for you what I always was—your love—and will be, for ever more.'

'Our two hearts sworn on it?'

'I must go,' she said more faintly, her warmth leaving him, 'but it'll be all right, yes. I swear it on my heart, it'll be all right, all right, all right, my sweet darling.'

But when she had gone he had this mortal blackness in him and was left with all the frightful trouble of his soul. It twisted in him as he lay on the bed, as sharp as what you die of. What could he do but clutch at the bedrails like a madman and beg for revenge and death? There you saw, Kleber, a tough man, wrestling with problems beyond his strength and far beyond any solution he could hope for, and that was what he babbled out in his greying mind.

Yet presently he passed into the state that a tortured man calls sleep and managed to sleep as day grew slowly out of her own shadow, the night, light with its own unerring magic emerging from the dark, and he came reluctantly back to life for yet another day after dreaming and yearning for Elenya, after seeing her in his sleep arriving at his bed, more beautiful, tall and proud than he had ever seen her, dressed in dark red, a dress he had never known her wear, its skirts trailing around her white feet as though driven by the wind—and it was as though, in that dream he had just had of her, it was some amazing gift she had presented to him against his loss of her that enabled him to get out of bed and continue, that enabled him somehow to carry on. For how could such beauty as hers ever be known to one who was not dying for it, and willing to die? All errors, births, ill luck and catastrophes were now cancelled out by that dream he had had of her.

There were instants when he believed that he and Elenya would never die; for people like themselves would always be in the presence of being born again, so it was almost, it seemed to him, as if he and Elenya would be them: at least please God it might be so. Even if not, he would be happy as long as they were together somewhere, or even nowhere. But they must be together, that was all, because she was his love, his only sweetheart, and his other self. Even when she had been alive, Kleber (knowing that the more you loved someone the more precious they were to you, the more fragile they could be) had sometimes tried to imagine, to picture to himself, what the loss of her would involve, but each time he had given up the task as hopeless, for he was far too close to her to be able to think about her objectively—although there were times, when he looked in the mirror to shave, when it was her face he expected to see there, not his own.

Immediately he thought this Elenya was beside him to whisper: 'Mark's here.'

'I've let you down, Mark,' said Kleber. 'Everyone I loved and liked best in the world seems to have died because of me.'

'You mustn't think like that. You must join us; it's wonderful over here.'

'Will I really be all right, do you think? Will I really see her again?'

'Of course you will.'

'But I'm afraid of getting lost. How shall I get to you?'

'We'll see to that.'

'Listen to him, my love,' whispered Elenya. 'He's right. Listen to what he says, your friend.'

'We're here,' said Mark, 'and because you believe in us, and we in you, we always will be.'

Kleber heard Elenya say to Mark: 'It shouldn't have been allowed. I don't understand why it was allowed.'

'We're only young dead,' said Mark. 'There are matters we don't understand yet.'

Elenya said: 'I love him as though he were eternity itself.'

'It's getting to you,' said Kleber. 'That's what worries me so. Reaching you.'

'Trust us,' said Mark. 'There'll just be a short black moment, and then we'll lead you safely through to us.'

'Yes, darling, there's a way,' said Elenya, and he felt her hand stroke his face as his mother used to when he had had an accident and hurt himself.

'Elenya,' he said, but there was a sudden silence. For Kleber, the silence was like being taken out and shot against a wall.

*

Only the other night Elenya had said to him in her sleep: 'Hold me, hold me, yes, there, up there to the mirror of the dark, and together we'll defeat the night.' She had thrown her hot arms around him in her dreams, and he had held her body. He had held her absolutely to him in her sleep, and now he knew that it was because she had already prefigured her end, though at that time, of course, he hadn't understood.

When she woke up she yawned and kissed him, saying: 'I love you. I love you so.'

He felt the sweetness of her thighs against him. 'Oh, God,' he said, kissing her between her shoulders, 'you're the most wonderful experience I could have had, my darling, or ever could have. The idea of ever losing you troubles me so greatly that I never dare think about it.'

'Don't be such a fool,' she murmured, running her fingers through his hair. 'You couldn't lose me if you wanted to. No one could ever replace you for me. If you did get lost, I'd always find a way of reaching you—now don't worry, darling.'

The marvel of love that cannot be stolen by the envious or the stupid.

'Death itself couldn't separate us, sweetheart,' she said, 'and now I want you to come into me like that—yes, like that, my diamond.'

And so he remembered how he had made love with her that night that was now like a thousand years ago and how he had been crying that time with his passion for her, just as, alone, he was crying now.

Now he went to sit for a time in the punch-drunk armchair that had half its seat missing and think about her. It was on the back of the same armchair that he had seen her hand resting.

Now suddenly she was there, just outside the door. 'Oh, won't you come to me?' she said.

'But darling, I'm here.'

'I'm in pieces, in death and unquiet, and I want you now.'

'Come then, sweet one, here I am.'

'But I can't get through, my own heart; I can't get through the door.'

'But it's open! I never lock it because of you.'

'It's not that,' she said in her sweet sadness. 'I can go through walls and time if I'm allowed.' In his mind he saw her beautiful face that tried to smile at him entreatingly, only all her teeth were gone and her mouth was full of earth. 'Help me, darling,' she whispered. 'I'm so cold suddenly and I can't see you. I think I've gone blind.'

'Here, sweet one,' said Kleber, 'I'll be all you need to warm you, my only, only love—I'll be your eyes, I'll be your everything.'

'Why do we have to come and go like this?' she said. 'What's happened, and why?' She said, 'Here's my hand,' and he saw her hand come out to him, her left hand, the one that the police had picked up in the garden. He touched it, and it was ice cold from the morgue. He moaned: 'Oh, Christ. What am I here for now?'

She shook her head sadly: 'You were spared only to die, my sweet prince, and it seems there is a reason behind it, although I can't remember what it is just now.'

Was violence on earth, Kleber wondered later, anything to do with that level of understanding? The understanding they had? Well, it was no good worrying now, he thought. I shouldn't have lost her; it's too late now. And then he thought savagely: No, it isn't too late. It's never, never too late. I'll get her back. Somehow everything will be exactly as it was before, only the next time I won't make any mistakes.

He remembered how, one night in summer when they were making love, she had kissed him all over his body, and he wrung his disaster-stricken hands.

In the Bar Tahiti a man came up to Kleber and said: 'There are some people who run this district who think it might be a good thing if you were killed.' He was a heavy man, a little on the stout side. 'You're making too many waves.'

Kleber shrugged over his glass without bothering to look at the man. 'You've none of you ever been in love,' he said.

At that very minute the man Kleber was after said to the killer he usually hired: 'OK, there's only one to go now. Kleber. I'm sick and tired of the cunt.'

'Right.'

'Don't worry about money. How'll you do it?'

'Shotgun, I like them best. It goes off with a better bang than I can get in my pants.'

'Here's five hundred thousand on account, the rest when it's done. You can get going.'

'I'll see you here tomorrow, same time. It'll be done by then.'

'He shouldn't have got up my nose,' the man whom Kleber was after said, 'but these things can't be helped. Bye-bye.'

*

The first night Kleber ever took Elenya home with him to his flat he said to her: 'I feel most strange. I think I must be in love with you. I *am* in love with you.'

She took him to the bed and said: 'I know. Take me, Kleber.'

And he did take her.

And now look what had happened.

'What are you talking about,' the stout man in the bar was saying to Kleber, 'love? Are you ill or what?'

'Yes, love lost is the tragedy that knows no frontiers,' Kleber said.

'Why don't you just go away and get out of everyone's hair?'

But Kleber, who wasn't looking at him anyway, didn't answer, because he was in a different world. He was in a state of love that had been transmuted into a strange new form. It was so ancient that to him it was brand new and brilliantly lit; it swept tenderly towards him, smiling into his eyes so profoundly as it came, opening its arms as it did so, that he wanted to give his life for it, knowing that it would willingly do the same for him. Death is the only transformer, he thought—but we had to live first to know it.

He thought he had probably never grown up much after sixteen. He had grown up in his brain but not his heart, where he had been so profoundly struck. His was a deeply reasoning head coupled to the heart of an adolescent's tenderness and anxieties. Elenya's death had not altered the meaning of reality in him, as happened with the mad. The streets were still there all right; it was only that he no longer had any motive to observe them, as he had once taken such pleasure in doing and then, because of his career, had to. But, without Elenya, nothing meant anything to him now; it was no more fun.

'I'm telling you,' the heavy man said.

Kleber said: 'Go away. Fuck off.'

'It won't end there,' said the man.

'I won't tell you twice,' Kleber said.

Vast questions. He still looked for the pieces of what life should have been in the night while they were alive. As always in our existence they had somehow searched and found each other's hands in the dark, and couldn't see why they had to do it again. All Kleber wondered and wanted to know was why his life had seemed to him to be so short, yet his pain so long? He prayed it might never be repeated.

'Oh, darling,' said Elenya suddenly, 'hold me in your arms so that I can see into the mirror of the night with you.'

'Where are you, my only darling?'

'Don't you feel my arm around your waist?'

My sweet little star, my love, my other self, Kleber said, I understand that you and I are broken, and yet we can never be broken, holding to each other as strongly as we do. In our intentions we love and hold for others, as we all must if we aren't to rot. Since my loss of you I see the clear image of the grave in my own face, and love is heavy in me, but it's a general love, and because of it we shall never die. The bores of this earth think that we have both been thrown over by them, but that will never happen. Our pale white crowns are still in place, and as long as we both believe, each in our own world, they always will be. I see now that when I used to kiss your body, I kissed every body in the world.

The man Kleber was looking for lay back in his armchair, waiting for results. He didn't look good in early daylight—he didn't look good in any light, come to that. He bulged at the waist and was growing bald; he had liver spots on the backs of his hands. He sat back listening to bad rock music, his big fat cock leaning sideways from his trousers where he could fondle it; it looked strange between the parting of the zip in his pink-checked suit. He started playing with the thing, and it looked up at him from its narrow pink hole. As usual he had half a hard on, never a full one, which was why he loathed women and could only get a proper hard-on when he raped them.

The telephone rang: the man got up to answer it with his cock hanging down.

'Good,' he said, when he has listened to the message from Kleber's killer. 'Yes, that's excellent.'

It felt to Kleber like a real arm about his body, which was all the more terrible for him since he had seen the pieces of her hanging in the bushes and had waited to see the firemen hosing her blood down the drain. He had stayed to watch what they could find of her packed up by the police and then put into their van—her left hand and one of her cheeks he had seen being packed. When the van turned the corner, he felt as if he had been left behind for all eternity, and found himself echoing inside with frightful cries—frightful internal cries that bled him slowly to death when he would rather have had done with it by a single stab wound and then, being free, be able to rush off and find her; but until he did find her that faintness of leaking blood inside him would never end.

He was in a bar, and even as he knew that he believed he saw her. The place had two large windows with the door in between, and Kleber was sitting on a stool, his back to the bar, facing the wet street. He didn't see her come past either of the windows but saw her at the door. She was wearing the blue dress he had given her on her last birthday, but she had no coat on; she seemed oblivious to the rain. She didn't stop at the door of the bar but turned her face to him as she passed—it was very white and she went on, moving quickly, with a half-smile, and was gone. It was over in a second, yet Kleber absorbed every detail of her, from her face to her shoes, which he remembered them buying together (they were a blue and white pair); the suddenness of her, as well as the sight of her lost beauty, gave him such a shock that he thought he was going to fall and nearly did.

A stout young man sitting next to Kleber turned to him and said: 'Have you got a light on you by any chance?'

'What?' said Kleber, returning to this world and going through his pockets. 'Yes, here.'

The young man nudged him. 'You look pale, if you don't mind my saying so. Are you all right?'

'I'm all right.' He said to the barman: 'I'll have an Armagnac; make it a double.'

'All right,' said the barman, 'but make it quick.'

When he brought it, Kleber downed it in one swallow and said: 'How's that?'

'Who cares?' said the barman.

'I do,' said Kleber. 'Have you seen my man?'

'What man? I don't know what you're talking about, and I don't want to.'

The phone rang behind the barman and he answered it. He listened, nodded, rang off and said to Kleber: 'That'll be twenty-one francs.'

Kleber put money on the bar but the young man put his hand on Kleber's and said quickly: 'No, no, this is on me.' He gave the barman a fifty-franc note and pushed Kleber's money back to him.

'Two people in love,' said the barman, looking at them.

'You're no help to anyone really, are you?' said Kleber. 'You ought to wipe your mouth out with a dirty sponge, you cunt.'

'You're pushing your luck,' said the barman.

'No, I'm not,' said Kleber, 'but you would be if you tried to push yours—it might go straight off the edge of the plate, darling, especially in this district. You need a little more of our training, don't you? I can see you're a country boy trying to come on like a big city man, so I warn you that around here the treatment's sharp and painful. Now keep quiet, do you understand?'

The barman understood.

'Good,' said Kleber. 'Now fuck off and work your bad manners off on someone else.'

He said to the young man: 'Why's this round on you? I don't even know you.' Kleber was in the middle of taking the worst risk of all—walking into the loneliness and danger of his own soul with no help but from the invisible and lost.

'Who's the man you're after?' asked the youth beside him slyly. 'A boyfriend?'

'Hardly,' said Kleber. 'Now look, all I want is to sit here and drink my drink and be left alone, do you mind?'

'I bought you this one,' said the young man, edging closer to Kleber. 'Surely that gives me the right to some conversation with you?'

'It doesn't,' said Kleber. 'Twenty-one francs doesn't give anybody the right to anything.' He said to the barman: 'Bring me another Armagnac.'

'Aren't you going to buy me one?' said the young man.

'No,' said Kleber.

'Not even a beer? I'm thirsty.'

'No,' said Kleber. 'What I'm going to give you instead is some extremely good advice—get out of here.'

'But I find you interesting.'

'I'm telling you for your own good,' said Kleber. 'Get right away from me. I'm bad news. Find some other bar and forget you ever saw me.'

The young man wanted to argue but then looked into Kleber's face and decided not to. He got up, struggled into his macintosh and went sadly out into the rain.

Out there, in the street, a man sitting in a parked car opposite straightened up to look at him bleakly, then relaxed in his seat with the shotgun in his arms; he held it as tenderly as he would a child.

The bar was empty except for an old man asleep over a wine glass.

'I'm closing now,' said the barman, 'so finish your drink and leave.'

'You're very cheeky,' said Kleber. 'Some people never learn.'

'Don't argue,' said the barman. 'I don't want any bother with the law. Now drink up and get lost.'

'Your manners are really frightful,' said Kleber, 'and that nice new jacket you've got on might have to go to the cleaners by the time I've finished with you, which would be fast. Blood's such difficult stuff to get out of clothes, don't you find?'

'I've never thought about it.'

'Start now,' said Kleber. At the same time he was remembering the first winter that he and Elenya had been married, and how they had gone to the countryside and into the white snow, each with an arm around the waist of the other, kissing and laughing with joy. They had walked a long way and their faces had been hot and red in spite of the frost, and then they had had breakfast at a little inn—eggs, wine and bread, some coffee. He said to the barman: 'Where's the back way out of here?'

'There isn't one,' said the barman. 'You just go out through the street door, the same one that other folk use.'

'You haven't got a back door?'

'No.'

'Then you're breaking the law,' said Kleber. 'This place is a firetrap.' But then he realised that the whole place was a trap.

'Why don't you report it, then?' the barman sneered.

'Because that isn't my way of doing things; I do it directly, my style.'

'No one's got any style much at this time of night.'

'You'd be surprised,' said Kleber. He crossed the bar and pushed the door open. He went out into the street and, as he did so, a terrific gust of wind blew every dead leaf high into the air on crazy vortices.

The barman locked the door behind Kleber and turned the lights out. Kleber thought, putting his face to the wind, the king's asleep and there are no princes left: he couldn't imagine where he had learned such a thing, or whether he had dreamed it.

*

Out in the street Kleber felt much calmer than he ought to have done, considering that he was sure of what was going to happen to him. He felt as a seriously ill man would feel while being taken into an operating theatre under a heavy sedative. He knew he was no longer part of life and he was even happy in an indescribable way because Elenya, although she wasn't with him just at that second, still seemed to him to be nearby: he could almost smell the peach-like scent of her cheeks. In spite of the vile weather he felt airy on his feet, and quite light in a part of himself that he didn't really know.

Yet he was still practical.

'I can hear you knocking, darling,' Kleber said.

'I'm everywhere around you,' she said, 'but I just can't get in.'

'This is a nightmare,' Kleber said, 'except that I'm awake.' But the music she made in his head was so old that he had trouble understanding it. 'Just come back,' he said.

She was knocking in his head, his memory and their past.

Kleber knew that you played your heart out to someone, and only once. There was a horrible storm going on in his mind. He staggered on in the wind in the wake of his own tragedy. It was a question of how anyone felt in front of finality, and Kleber was frightened of it because it was so close, but Elenya said: 'I'm here, darling; I'll protect you.'

Sébastopol was deserted almost, because of the cold; there was just the wind, which threw the naked trees into each others' arms. On each side of the boulevard stood lines of parked cars, the rain streaming off them.

'I've lost the battle,' Kleber said to himself. 'We all of us lose the battle in the end.' He knew that walking slowly up the boulevard on his own at that moment was stupid, but he didn't know what else to do, perhaps because for him there wasn't an alternative. He glanced up at the windows around him; he heard an all-night party going on behind two lighted ones. He envied the people—how he envied them! There must be young couples in love up there dancing, with a whole future in front of them, talking, communicating, with every conceivable reason for living in each others' arms. He sensed that he ought to cross the boulevard this minute and get back to his hotel, but for some reason he couldn't name he didn't and instead stood stock still. The odd taxi, car, fled down the murdered surface of the boulevard and Kleber watched them go, thinking of taxis he had taken with Elenya, her arms full of parcels. He thought about the three men he had shot the day before Elenya's death; he thought back to the meals he had had with Mark, and what good friends they had been.

Kleber stood on the pavement, feeling drained of his strength at last, his eyes sly, yet indifferent and half-closed, as the eyes of the dead look, and it was while he was gazing up the pavement to see if there was any sign of Elenya through the rain that the killer, who had got out of his parked car, aimed the shotgun at Kleber's heart and fired the buckshot into it. Because of the wind and the rain, the shotgun made little more sound than a fart at a dinner party—but the effect on Kleber wasn't the same thing at all; there was nothing polite about his reaction to half his body having gone. The shock hurled him into the plate-glass window of the closed bar as hard as if he had been knocked down by a truck and thrown along the length of a short street.

*

There had been a time when Kleber was a small boy that he had reached up to the fruit in trees, not to eat it but to give it away. And once, when he was describing to Elenya what this had meant to him, she had said: 'You know, sweet, I hardly ever criticise you, but if I were to, I would say that there are times when you think too much.'

And Kleber remembered that he had answered at that time: 'The kind of work I do, how can I help it? We do try to help people, you know, not just fuck them up.'

'As long as you know what you're doing,' Elenya said, 'it's all right.'

But had it been?

'Why do you work in the police?' she asked him once.

And all he could think of to say to her was: 'My darling, why have any of us ever done the work we have?'

'By necessity.'

'All right,' he said, 'I agree. But my greatest necessity is for justice.'

'Mine too,' she said, 'in my way,' and took his head and hid it between her little breasts until love came to save them from their sleep.

He had followed his parents up the rough stones of small paths as a little peasant when he had been a boy, and he and Mark had thrown idiotic things at each other on the way to their parents' work and been happy—he remembered that as he died.

A nice job, the killer thought as he dismantled his gun and packed its pieces away into their case. He put this under the driver's seat of his car. At least we never knew each other, he thought. He smiled; he had been paid. He took a brief professional look at Kleber's body lying practically cut in two, started up his stolen Fiat diesel and sped away.

It wasn't the *mairie*. In his dreams Kleber had married Elenya in a church. It was a pretty rotten church—that's to say, its roof was rotten and the place was in the country and the church was probably twelfth century. That didn't make any difference, though. Elenya was always, for ever, stretching out to him the gloved hand in white with the fourth finger ring that only princesses may wear in emeralds and diamonds, which hand he kissed as she gave herself to him in a great mass. She was incredibly beautiful that day and was given gently to him by kings and princes, who knew how to be generous as well as he did. So that there was still justice on the earth. Kleber ignored the sports and the spotty bores who turn up for any spectacle, especially if there's a free drink after it, and looked in the intensity of his love out of the plain windows of the church towards the fields, which seemed to him to become brighter in colour as he looked at them and to be shrinking away at the same time. She was so slender in her miraculous white that he could hardly start for tears, and ignored everyone but her. He was afraid his heart might burst with love for her before they could be alone, or else that life would change before they could both slip away. She smiled at him in the manner that she had only for him, and he answered her with his looks in the same way. She was a true beauty, pale, turning swiftly towards him on her heel, gazing at him from behind the depth of her eyes. Fools looked on it as just a marriage; it was impossible to get them to understand what their union meant, and Kleber didn't try—it was effort and time wasted. She came towards him for everything he had to give her, and then the priest was about to unite them...

Then, as always in that dream, she suddenly collapsed. She turned white; her teeth fell out of her head and appalling ruptures appeared on her face and breast. Terrible things happened to her in the dream, so that when he awoke and found her still in his arms, breathing, deeply asleep, he was so grateful that she was there that he kissed her and asked no more than that she could continue as she was, and she would turn and murmur in her own dreams. He used to kiss her all over her body in his gratitude for her, any part of her that he could reach and find; and so, through her, he was lifted from his sleep and life and connected to her in a way that he never completely understood until she died.

'Come back! Come back!' she used to shout at him in her dreams.

He used to soothe her, holding her tight in his arms: 'I'm coming, darling.'

'No, but come back!'

'I'm here. I've never been away.' Whereon she would usually wake up and look at him with huge eyes still half-drowned in sleep and say: 'Was I dreaming? Had you really gone?'

'As if I ever could.'

'But I dreamed that—'

'It was only a dream, darling.'

'Dreams can be so real, though.'

'They can seem real enough, I admit.'

'You'd never really let go of me, would you? I dreamed you had. It's my worst dream.'

'Never would I do that.'

The last thing he remembered before he died was the impossibility of the damage that had been done to him long before the killer had blown him in two. The last conscious thought he had was about cunts—how one cunt is always unkind to another. Cunts are always peering about looking for money, usually in the divorce courts or out of boredom; no cunt ever kneels to a princess's ring. Cunts adore money; princes won't touch it even if it costs them their head; a prince never scrambles. Money disgusts a prince or a peasant, because the first is usually born of the second and is only peculiar because he wears gloves.

So life and death, like any bad or meaningless experience or dream, was just a hideous fairy tale with no kind uncle in the wings.

Three of Kleber's uncles had been killed far back in the Second World War, and all Kleber wanted to do was to take Elenya by the waist and join them. He had been told that it would not be very easy since the obvious never is, but he didn't care; he wanted her—wanted to get back into his little world.

It cost a single barrel from a twelve-bore—and his wishes were all granted, and he remembered in the hundredth of a second that it took him to die that in the last two days that she had been dead, her voice had sounded false and feverish as she called for him to come back to her, as if she had been running a high temperature in a world where there was nothing and no one to cure her.

You also think so quickly even when you're dying that he thought of death in the terms of a beautiful woman waving goodbye to a quay from the afterdeck of what was known to be a doomed steamer.

He survived for a time until his luck and Elenya's ran out.

None of it mattered now. He lay sprawled in his blood on the pavement of Sébastopol under the pouring rain, every idea that had ever been in his head running away into the gutter with it.

But then a miracle occurred, though there was no one on the street to see it. As Kleber lay on the pavement, a light appeared far up the street which, as it got closer to Kleber's body in the shape first of a brilliant blue, white and gold ball shot through with lightning, and then of Elenya, hurrying to get to him. The moment she was beside him she became radiant, dressed entirely in white, with a smile of joy on her face as she leaned to support him that people never see on this earth. She was now of a sublime beauty not of this world, spreading over them both an understanding that cannot be known our side of mortality. She bent over Kleber's corpse with the endless love she had to give and took him by the hands until he, too, rose from his soaked and bloody remains to assume her own brilliance—and so, holding each other by the waist, gazing into each other's eyes and speaking again at last, unheard by the sleeping planet, they walked to the corner of a little street, turned into it and disappeared.

And so, you see, there was some love left in the world after all.

Other Derek Raymond titles of interest and published by Serpent's Tail

He Died with His Eyes Open
(the first of the Factory series of novels)

When a middle-aged alcoholic is found brutally battered to death on a roadside in West London, the case is assigned to a nameless detective sergeant, a tough-talking cynic and fearless loner from the Department of Unexplained Deaths at the Factory police station. Working from cassette tapes left behind in the dead man's property, our narrator must piece together the history of his blighted existence and discover the agents of its cruel end. What he doesn't expect is that digging for the truth will demand plenty of lying, and that the most terrible of villains will also prove to be the most attractive.

In the first of six police procedurals that comprise the Factory series, Derek Raymond spins a riveting, and vividly human crime drama. Relentlessly pursuing justice for the dispossessed, his detective narrator treads where few others dare: in the darkest corners of London, a city of sin plagued by unemployment, racism and vice, and peopled by a cast of low-lifes, all utterly convincing and brought to life by Raymond's pitch-perfect dialogue.

The Crust on its Uppers

'It's a tale of someone who wanted to go and go-who was sick of the dead-on-its-feet upper crust he was born into, that he didn't believe in, didn't want, whose values were meaningless, that did nothing but hold him back from his first nanny onwards. I wanted to chip my way out of that background which held me like a flea in a block of ice, and crime was the only chisel I could find.'

First published in 1962, *The Crust on Its Uppers*, Derek Raymond's first novel (written when he was Robin Cook) is a gripping tale of class betrayal. With ruthless precision, it brings vividly to life a Britain of spivs, crooked toffs and bent coppers – in fact, a Britain that in its bare essentials has changed little over the last 30 years.

'Best place to start is the slangy baroque of the re-issued *The Crust On Its Uppers*, Raymond's autobiographical account of the dodgy transactions between high class wide boys and low class villains. You won't read a better novel about 60s London' *i-D*

'Tremendous black comedy of Chelsea gangland, written and set in the early Sixties, on the cusp of swinging London' *The Face*

'A breathlessly good read, as funny, relevant and resonant at it was thirty years ago' *Literary Review*

'Peopled by a fast-talking shower of queens, spades, morries, slags, shysters, grifters and grafters of every description, it is one of the great London novels' *New Statesman*

A State of Denmark

England is ruled by Jobling, a dictator with an efficient secret police and a long memory.

Richard Watt used all his journalistic talents to expose Jobling before he came to power. Now, in exile in Italy, Watt cultivates his vineyards. His rural idyll is shattered by the arrival of an emissary from London... Derek Raymond's deft skill is to make all too plausible the transition to dictatorship in an England obssessed with 'looking after number one' First published in 1970, *A State of Denmark* is a classic.

'Raymond's novel is rooted firmly in the dystopian vision of Orwell and Huxley, sharing their air of horrifying hopelessness' *Sunday Times*

'*A State of Denmark* is carried out with surgical precision... a fascinating and important novel by one of our best writers in or outside of any genre' *Time Out*

'Alternative science fiction on the scale of Orwell's *1984* or Zamyatin's *We*' Q

Fiction
Non-fiction
Literary
Crime

Popular culture
Biography
Illustrated
Music

dare to read at serpentstail.com

Visit serpentstail.com today to browse and buy our
books, and for exclusive previews, promotions,
interviews with authors and forthcoming events.

NEWS — cut to the literary chase with all the latest news about our books and authors

EVENTS — advance information on forthcoming events, author readings, exhibitions and book festivals

EXTRACTS — read first chapters, short stories, bite-sized extracts

EXCLUSIVES — pre-publication offers, signed copies, discounted books, competitions

BROWSE AND BUY — browse our full catalogue, fill up a basket and proceed to our **fully secure** checkout - our website is your oyster

FREE POSTAGE & PACKING ON ALL ORDERS ANYWHERE!

---

sign up today and receive our new free full colour catalogue